HORRID HENRY

12 STORIES OF CHRISTMAS

FRANCESCA SIMON

FRANCESCA SIMON SPENT HER CHILDHOOD ON THE BEACH IN CALIFORNIA AND STARTED WRITING STORIES AT THE AGE OF EIGHT. SHE WROTE HER FIRST HORRID HENRY BOOK IN 1994. HORRID HENRY HAS GONE ON TO CONQUER THE GLOBE; HIS ADVENTURES HAVE SOLD MILLIONS OF COPIES WORLDWIDE.

FRANCESCA HAS WON THE CHILDREN'S BOOK OF THE YEAR AWARD AND IN 2009 WAS AWARDED A GOLD BLUE PETER BADGE. SHE WAS ALSO A TRUSTEE OF THE WORLD BOOK DAY CHARITY FOR SIX YEARS.

FRANCESCA LIVES IN NORTH LONDON WITH HER FAMILY.

WWW.FRANCESCASIMON.COM
WWW.HORRIDHENRY.CO.UK
@SIMON_FRANCESCA

TONY ROSS

TONY ROSS WAS BORN IN LONDON AND STUDIED AT THE LIVERPOOL SCHOOL OF ART AND DESIGN. HE HAS WORKED AS A CARTOONIST, A GRAPHIC DESIGNER, AN ADVERTISING ART DIRECTOR AND A UNIVERSITY LECTURER.

TONY IS ONE OF THE MOST POPULAR AND SUCCESSFUL CHILDREN'S ILLUSTRATORS OF ALL TIME, BEST KNOWN FOR ILLUSTRATING HORRID HENRY AND THE WORKS OF DAVID WALLIAMS, AS WELL AS HIS OWN HUGELY POPULAR SERIES, THE LITTLE PRINCESS. HE LIVES IN MACCLESFIELD.

HORRID HENRY

12 STORIES OF CHRISTMAS

FRANCESCA SIMON

ILLUSTRATED BY TONY ROSS

Orion

ORION CHILDREN'S BOOKS

Stories originally published in "Horrid Henry: Get Rich Quick", "Horrid Henry: Bogey Babysitter", "Horrid Henry: Stinkbombs!", "Horrid Henry: Football Fiend", "Horrid Henry: Christmas Cracker", "Horrid Henry: Abominable Snowman", "Horrid Henry: Cannibal Curse" and "Horrid Henry: Up, Up and Away" respectively.

This collection first published in Great Britain in 2022 by
Hodder & Stoughton

1 3 5 7 9 10 8 6 4 2

Text © Francesca Simon 1998, 2002, 2006, 2007, 2015, 2019
Illustrations © Tony Ross 1998, 2002, 2006, 2007, 2015, 2019

The rights of Francesca Simon and Tony Ross to be identified as author and illustrator of this work have been asserted.

A CIP catalogue record for this book is available from the British Library.

ISBN 978 1 51011 089 2

Printed and bound in Great Britain by Clays Ltd, Elcograf S.P.A.

The paper and board used in this book are from well-managed forests and other responsible sources.

MIX
Paper from
responsible sources
FSC® C104740
www.fsc.org

Orion Children's Books
An imprint of
Hachette Children's Group
Part of Hodder & Stoughton
Carmelite House
50 Victoria Embankment
London EC4Y 0DZ

An Hachette UK Company
www.hachette.co.uk

www.hachettechildrens.co.uk
www.horridhenry.co.uk

CONTENTS

HORRID HENRY'S

CHRISTMAS PLAY

A cold dark day in November
(37 days till Christmas)

Horrid Henry *slumped* on the carpet and willed the clock to go faster. Only five more minutes to hometime! Already Henry could taste those **CRISPS** he'd be sneaking from the cupboard.

MISS BATTLE-AXE droned on about *school dinners* (**YUCK**), the new drinking fountain BLAH BLAH BLAH, maths homework BLAH BLAH BLAH, the school

Christmas play BLAH BLAH BLAH . . . what?
Did Miss Battle-Axe say . . . Christmas
play? Horrid Henry sat up.

"This is a brand-new play with
singing and DANCING," continued Miss
Battle-Axe. "And both the older and
the younger children are taking part
this year."

Singing! DANCING! Showing off in
front of the whole school! Years ago,
when Henry was in the infants' class,
he'd the played eighth sheep in the
nativity play and had SNATCHED the
baby from the manger and refused

to hand him back. Henry hoped **MISS BATTLE-AXE** wouldn't remember.

Because Henry had to play the lead. He had to. Who else but Henry could be an all-singing, **ALL-DANCING** Joseph?

"I want to be Mary," shouted every girl in the class.

"I want to be a wise man!" shouted Rude Ralph.

"I want to be a sheep!" shouted Anxious Andrew.

"I want to be Joseph!" shouted Horrid Henry.

"No, me!" shouted Jazzy Jim.

"**ME!**" shouted Brainy Brian.

"**QUIET!**" shrieked **MISS BATTLE-AXE**. "I"m the director, and my decision about who will act which part is final. I've cast the play as follows: Margaret, you will be **MARY**." She handed her a thick script.

Moody Margaret *whooped* with joy. All the other girls glared at her.

"Susan, front legs of the **donkey**; Linda, hind legs; cows, Fiona and Clare. BLADES OF GRASS —" Miss Battle-Axe continued assigning parts.

Pick me for Joseph, pick

me for JOSEPH, Horrid Henry begged silently. Who better than the best actor in the school to play the starring part?

"I'm a sheep, I'm a sheep, I'm a beautiful sheep!" warbled Singing Soraya.

"I'm a **SHEPHERD!**" beamed Jolly Josh.

"I'm an angel,"

trilled Magic Martha.

"I'm a BLADE OF GRASS," sobbed Weepy William.

"Joseph will be played by—"

"ME!" screamed Henry.

"Me!" screamed New Nick, Greedy Graham, Dizzy Dave and Aerobic Al.

"Peter," said Miss Battle-Axe. "From Miss Lovely's class."

Horrid Henry felt as if he'd been *slugged* in the stomach. Perfect Peter?

His younger brother? Perfect Peter
gets the starring part?

"**It's not fair!**" howled Horrid
Henry.

MISS BATTLE-AXE *glared* at him.

"Henry, you're—" Miss Battle-Axe
consulted her list. Please not a BLADE
OF GRASS, please not a BLADE OF GRASS, prayed
Horrid Henry, shrinking. That would
be just like Miss Battle-Axe, to
humiliate him. Anything but that—

"—the INNKEEPER."

The INNKEEPER! Horrid Henry sat up,
beaming. How stupid he'd been:

the INNKEEPER must be the starring part.

Henry could see himself now,
polishing glasses, *throwing* darts,
pouring out big foaming FIZZYWIZZ
drinks to all his happy customers
while singing a song about the joys
of innkeeping. Then he'd get into a
nice long argument about why there
was NO ROOM AT THE INN, and finally,
the chance to **SLAM** the door in Moody
Margaret's face after he'd *pushed*
her away. Wow. Maybe he'd even get
a second song. "**Ten Green Bottles**"
would fit right into the story: he'd

sing and **DANCE** while knocking his
less talented classmates off a wall.
Wouldn't that be **FUN!**

MISS BATTLE-AXE handed a page to
Henry. "Your script," she said.

Henry was puzzled. Surely there
were some pages missing?

He read:

(Joseph knocks. The innkeeper opens the door.)

JOSEPH: Is there any room at the inn?

INNKEEPER: No.

(The innkeeper shuts the door.)

Horrid Henry turned over the page. It was blank. He held it up to the light.

There was no secret writing. That was it.

His entire part was **one line**. One

stupid puny line. Not even a line, a word. "No."

Where was his song? Where was his **DANCE** with the bottles and the guests at the inn? How could he, **Horrid Henry**, the best actor in the class (and indeed, the **WORLD**) be given just one word in the school play? Even the **donkeys** got a song.

Worse, after he said his one word, Perfect Peter and Moody Margaret got to yack for hours about mangers and wise men and shepherds and sheep, and then sing a duet, while he, Henry,

hung about behind the hay with the
BLADES OF GRASS.

It was so unfair!

He should be the star of the show,
not his **stupid worm** of a brother. Why
on earth was Peter cast as Joseph
anyway? He was a **TERRIBLE**
actor. He couldn't sing, he just squeaked
like a squished toad. And why was
Margaret playing Mary? Now she'd
never stop bragging and swaggering.

AAARRRGGGGHHHH!

"Isn't it exciting!" said Mum.

"Isn't it thrilling!" said Dad. "Our little boy, the star of the show."

"Well done, Peter," said Mum.

"We're so proud of you," said Dad.

Perfect Peter smiled modestly.

"Of course I'm not really the star," he said. "Everyone's important, even little parts like the BLADES OF GRASS and the INNKEEPER."

Horrid Henry *pounced*. He was a
GREAT WHITE SHARK lunging for
the kill.

"AAAARRRRGGGHH!" squealed
Peter. "Henry bit me!"

"Henry! Don't be **HORRID!**" snapped
Mum.

"Henry! Go to your room!" snapped
Dad.

Horrid Henry **stomped** upstairs and
slammed the door. How could he bear
the humiliation of playing the INNKEEPER
when Peter was the star? He'd just
have to force Peter to switch roles with

him. Henry was sure he could find a way to persuade Peter, but persuading Miss Battle-Axe was a different matter. **MISS BATTLE-AXE** had a mean, HORRIBLE way of never doing what Henry wanted.

Maybe he could trick Peter into leaving the show. Yes! And then nobly offer to replace him.

But unfortunately, there was no guarantee Miss Battle-Axe would give Henry Peter's role. She'd probably just replace Peter with Goody-Goody Gordon. He was stuck.

And then Horrid Henry had a brilliant, SPECTACULAR idea. Why hadn't he thought of this before? If he couldn't play a bigger part, he'd just have to make his part **bigger**. For instance, he could SCREAM "**NO!**". That would get a reaction. Or he could bellow "**NO!**" and then hit Joseph. I'm an ANGRY INNKEEPER, thought Horrid Henry, and I hate guests coming to my inn. Certainly smelly ones like Joseph. Or he could shout "**NO!**", hit Joseph, then rob him. I'm a ROBBER INNKEEPER, thought Henry. Or, I'm a ROBBER pretending to be an **innkeeper**. That would liven up the play a bit. Maybe he could be a *French* **ROBBER** *innkeeper*, shout "**Non!**" and rob Mary and Joseph. Or he was a *French* **ROBBER PIRATE** INNKEEPER, so he could shout "**Non!**", tie Mary and Joseph up and make them walk the plank.

Hmmm, thought Horrid Henry. Maybe my part won't be so SMALL. After all, the *innkeeper* was the most important character.

12 December
(only 13 more days till Christmas)

Rehearsals had been going on for ever. **Horrid Henry** spent most of his time *slumping* in a chair. He'd never seen such a boring play.

Naturally he'd done everything he could to improve it.

"Can't I add a **DANCE?**" asked Henry.

"No," snapped Miss Battle-Axe.

"Can't I add a TEENY-WEENY-LITTLE song?" Henry pleaded.

"**NO!**" said Miss Battle-Axe.

"But how does the INNKEEPER know there's no room?" said Henry. "I think I should—"

MISS BATTLE-AXE *glared* at him with her red eyes.

"One more word from you, Henry, and you'll change places with Linda," snapped Miss Battle-Axe. "BLADES OF GRASS, let's try again . . ."

Eeek! An INNKEEPER with one word was infinitely better than being invisible as the hind legs of a **donkey**. Still — it was so unfair. He was only trying to help.

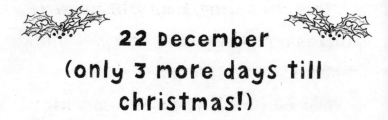

22 December
(only 3 more days till christmas!)

SHOWTIME! Not a tea towel was to be found in any local shop. Mums and

dads had been up all night frantically sewing costumes. Now the waiting and the rehearsing were over.

Everyone lined up on stage behind the curtain. Peter and Margaret waited on the side to make their **BIG** entrance as Mary and Joseph.

"Isn't it exciting, Henry, being in a real play?" whispered Peter.

"**NO**," snarled Henry.

"Places, everyone, for the opening song," hissed **MISS BATTLE-AXE**. "Now remember, don't worry if you make a LITTLE mistake: just carry on and

no one will notice."

"But I still think I should have an argument with Mary and Joseph about whether there's room," said Henry. "Shouldn't I at least check to see—"

"**NO!**" snapped Miss Battle-Axe,

glaring at him. "If I hear another PEEP from you, Henry, you will sit behind the bales of hay and Jim will play your part. BLADES OF GRASS! Line up with the **donkeys!** Sheep! Get ready to baaa . . . Bert! Are you a sheep or a BLADE OF GRASS?"

"I dunno," said Beefy Bert.

Mrs Oddbod went to the front of the stage. "Welcome, everyone, mums and dads, boys and girls, to our new Christmas play, a little different from previous years. We hope you all enjoy a brand-new show!"

MISS BATTLE-AXE started the CD player. The music pealed. The curtain rose. The audience **STAMPED** and *cheered*. Stars twinkled. Cows mooed. **Horses** neighed. Sheep baaed. Cameras flashed.

Horrid Henry stood in the wings and watched the shepherds do their

HIGHLAND DANCE. He still hadn't decided for sure how he was going to play his part. There were so many possibilities. It was so hard to choose.

Finally, Henry's **big moment** arrived.

He strode across the stage and waited behind the closed inn door for Mary and Joseph.

KNOCK KNOCK!

The *innkeeper* stepped forward and opened the door. There was Moody Margaret, simpering away as Mary, and Perfect Peter looking full of

himself as Joseph.

"Is there any room at the inn?" asked Joseph.

Good question, thought Horrid Henry. His mind was **BLANK**. He'd thought of so many GREAT THINGS he could say that what he was supposed to say had just gone straight out of his head.

"Is there any room at the inn?" repeated Joseph loudly.

"**YeS**," said the INNKEEPER. "Come on in."

Joseph *looked* at Mary.

Mary *looked* at Joseph.

The audience murmured.

OOpS, thought Horrid Henry. Now he remembered. He'd been supposed to say **no**. Oh well, in for a penny, in for a pound.

The INNKEEPER grabbed Mary and Joseph's sleeves and *yanked* them through the door. "Come on in, I haven't got all day."

"But . . . but . . . the inn's full," said Mary.

"No it isn't," said the INNKEEPER.

"Is too."

"Is *not*. It's my inn and I should know. This is the best inn in Bethlehem. We've got TVs and beds, and—" the INNKEEPER paused for a moment. What did inns have in them? "—and computers!"

Mary *glared* at the INNKEEPER.

The INNKEEPER *glared* at Mary.

Miss Battle-Axe gestured frantically from the wings.

"This inn looks full to me," said Mary firmly. "Come on, Joseph, let's go to the stable."

"Oh, don't go there, you'll get **fleas**," said the innkeeper.

"So?" said Mary.

"I love **fleas**," said Joseph weakly.

"And it's full of **MANURE**."

"So are you," snapped Mary.

"Don't be **horrid**, Mary," said the INNKEEPER severely. "Now sit down and rest your weary bones and I'll sing you a song." And the INNKEEPER started singing:

♪ ♫ ♪ ♩ ♫

"Ten green bottles, standing on a wall,
Ten green bottles, standing on a wall,
And if one green bottle should
accidentally fall—"

"**OOOHHH!**" moaned Mary. "I'm
having the baby."

"Can't you wait till I've finished my
song?" snapped the INNKEEPER.

"**NO!**" bellowed Mary.

MISS BATTLE-AXE drew her hand
across her throat.

Henry ignored her. After all, the
show must go on.

"Come on, Joseph," interrupted Mary. "We're going to the stable."

"Okay," said Joseph.

"You're making a **BIG MISTAKE**," said the INNKEEPER. "We've got **SATELLITE TV** and . . ."

Miss Battle-Axe ran on stage and nabbed him.

"Thank you, INNKEEPER, your other guests need you now," said Miss Battle-Axe, *grabbing* him by the collar.

"MERRY CHRISTMAS!"

shrieked Horrid Henry as she yanked him off-stage.

There was a very long silence.

"**BRAVO!**" yelled Moody Margaret's deaf aunt.

Mum and Dad weren't sure what to do. Should they clap, or run away to a place where no one knew them?

Mum clapped.

Dad hid his face in his hands.

"Do you think anyone noticed?" whispered Mum.

Dad looked at Mrs Oddbod's grim face. He **sank down** in his chair. Maybe one day he would learn how to make himself invisible.

"But what was I supposed to do?" said **Horrid Henry** afterwards in Mrs Oddbod's office. "It's not my fault I forgot my line. Miss Battle-Axe said not to worry if we made a mistake and just to carry on."

Could he help it if a star
was born?

HORRID HENRY

AND THE
ABOMINABLE
SNOWMAN

Moody Margaret took aim.

THWACK!

A snowball *whizzed* past and **SMACKED** Sour Susan in the face.

"**AAAAARRGGHHH!**" shrieked Susan.

"Ha ha, got you," said Margaret.

"You big meanie," howled Susan, scooping up a fistful of snow and *hurling* it at Margaret.

THWACK!

Susan's snowball **SMACKED** Moody Margaret in the face.

"**OWWWW!**" screamed Margaret.

"You've blinded me."

"Good!" screamed Susan.

"**I HATE YOU!**" shouted Margaret, shoving Susan.

"**I HATE YOU MORE!**" shouted Susan, pushing Margaret.

Splat! Margaret toppled into the snow.

Splat! Susan toppled into the snow.

"I'm going home to build my own snowman," sobbed Susan.

"Fine. I'll win without you," said Margaret.

"Won't!"

"Will! I'm going to win, **copycat**," shrieked Margaret.

"**I'M GOING TO WIN**," shrieked Susan. "I kept my best ideas secret."

"**win? win what?**" demanded Horrid Henry, stomping down his front steps in his snow boots and *swaggering* over. Henry could hear

the word **win** from miles away.

"Haven't you heard about the competition?" said Sour Susan. "The prize is—"

"**SHUT UP! DON'T TELL HIM,**" shouted Moody Margaret, packing snow on to her snowman's head.

WIN? COMPETITION? PRIZE? Horrid Henry's ears quivered. What secret were they trying to keep from him? Well, not for long. **Horrid Henry** was an expert at extracting information.

"Oh, the competition. I know all about that," lied Horrid Henry. "Hey, *great* snowman," he added, strolling casually over to Margaret's snowman and pretending to admire her work.

Now, what should he do? **Torture?** Margaret's ponytail was always a tempting target. And snow down her jumper would make her talk.

What about **BLACKMAIL?** He could spread some great rumours about Margaret at school. Or . . .

"Tell me about the competition or the **ICE GUY** gets it," said Horrid Henry suddenly, *leaping* over to the snowman and putting his hands

49

round its neck.

"You wouldn't dare," gasped Moody
Margaret.

Henry's mittened hands got ready to
PUSH.

"Bye bye, head," hissed Horrid Henry.
"Nice knowing you."

Margaret's snowman **wobbled**.

"**STOP!**" screamed Margaret. "I'll tell you. It doesn't matter 'cause you'll never ever win."

"Keep talking," said Horrid Henry warily, watching out in case Susan tried to ambush him from behind.

"**FROSTY FREEZE** are having a best snowman competition," said Moody Margaret, glaring. "The winner gets a year's **FREE** supply of ice cream. The judges will decide tomorrow morning. Now get away from my snowman."

Horrid Henry walked off in a daze, his jaw **dropping**. Margaret and Susan *pelted* him with SNOWBALLS but Henry didn't even notice. Free ice cream for a year direct from the FROSTY FREEZE Ice Cream factory. **Oh wow!** Horrid Henry couldn't believe it. Mum and Dad were so mean and **HORRIBLE** they hardly ever let him have ice cream. And when they did, they never ever let him put on his own

hot fudge

sauce and

whipped cream and sprinkles. Or even scoop the ice cream himself. Oh no.

Well, when he won the **BEST SNOWMAN COMPETITION** they couldn't stop him gorging on **Chunky Chocolate Fab Fudge Caramel Delight**, or Vanilla Whip Tutti-Frutti Toffee Treat. **Oh boy!** Henry could taste that glorious ice cream now. He'd **LIVE** on ice cream. He'd **BATHE** in ice cream. He'd **SLEEP** in ice cream. Everyone from school would turn up at his house when the **FROSTY FREEZE** truck arrived bringing his weekly barrels.

No matter how much they begged, **Horrid Henry** would send them all away. No way was he sharing a DROP of his precious ice cream with anyone.

And all he had to do was to build the BEST SNOWMAN in the neighbourhood. **Pah!** Henry's was sure to be the winner. He would build the **BIGGEST** SNOWMAN of all. And not just a SNOWMAN. A SNOWMAN with claws, and **HORNS**, and *fangs*. A VAMPIRE·DEMON·MONSTER SNOWMAN. An ABOMINABLE SNOWMAN. **Yes!**

Henry watched Margaret and Susan *rolling* snow and packing their saggy SNOWMAN. Ha. SNOW HEAP, more like.

"You'll never win with that," jeered Horrid Henry. "Your SNOWMAN is PATHETIC."

"Better than yours," snapped Margaret.

Horrid Henry rolled his eyes.

"Obviously, because I haven't started mine yet."

"We've got a big head start on you, so **HA HA HA**," said Susan. "We're building a BALLERINA SNOWGIRL."

"SHUT UP, SUSAN," screamed Margaret. A BALLERINA SNOWGIRL? What a stupid idea. If that was the best they could do, Henry was sure to win.

"Mine will be the **BIGGEST**, the **BEST**, the most **GIGANTIC** snowman ever seen," said Horrid Henry. "And much better than your stupid SNOW BABY."

"Fat chance," sneered Margaret.

"Yeah, Henry," sneered Susan. "Ours is the best."

"No way," said Horrid Henry, starting to roll a **GIGANTIC** ball of snow for ABOMINABLE'S BIG BELLY. There was no time to lose.

UP the path, down the path, across the garden, down the side, back and forth, back and forth, Horrid Henry

Roll.

Roll.

Roll.

rolled the **BIGGEST** ball of snow
ever seen.

"Henry, can I build a snowman with
you?" came a little voice.

"**NO**," said Henry, starting to carve
out some clawed feet.

"Oh please," said Peter. "We could
build a **GREAT BIG ONE** together. Like
a bunny snowman, or a—"

"No!" said Henry. "It's my
SNOWMAN. Build your own."

"Muuuummmm!" wailed Peter. "Henry
won't let me build a snowman with
him."

"Don't be **horrid**, Henry," said Mum.
"Why don't you build one together?"

"**NO!!!**" said Horrid Henry. He
wanted to make his own SNOWMAN.

If he built a SNOWMAN with his
stupid **worm** brother, he'd have to share
the prize. Well, no way. He wanted all
that ice cream for himself. And his
ABOMINABLE SNOWMAN was sure
to be the best. Why share a prize when
you didn't have to?

"Get away from my SNOWMAN,
Peter," hissed Henry.

Perfect Peter SNIVELLED. Then he started

to *roll* a tiny ball of snow.

"**AND GET YOUR OWN SNOW**," said
Henry. "All this is mine."

"Muuuuuum!" wailed Peter. "Henry's
hogging all the snow."

"We're done," trilled Moody Margaret.
"Beat this if you can."

Horrid Henry looked at Margaret
and Susan's SNOWGIRL, complete

with a big pink tutu wound round the
waist. It was as big as Margaret.

"That **old heap** of SNOW is

nothing compared to mine," bragged
Horrid Henry.

Moody Margaret and Sour Susan
looked at Henry's ABOMINABLE
SNOWMAN, complete with a Viking
horned helmet, fangs and HAIRY
SCARY CLAWS. It was a few
centimetres taller than Henry.

"**NAH NAH NE NAH NAH**, mine's bigger," boasted Henry.

"**NAH NAH NE NAH NAH**, mine's better," boasted Margaret.

"How do you like my snowman?" said Peter. "Do you think I could win?"

Horrid Henry stared at Perfect Peter's TINY snowman. It didn't even have a head, just a Long, thin, Lumpy body with two stones stuck in the top for eyes.

Horrid Henry howled with laughter.

"That's the **worst** SNOWMAN I've ever seen," said Henry. "It doesn't

even have a head. That's a SNOW
CARROT."

"It is not," wailed Peter. "It's a big
bunny."

"Henry! Peter! Suppertime," called
Mum.

Henry stuck out his tongue at
Margaret.

"And **DON'T YOU DARE** touch my
SNOWMAN."

Margaret stuck out her tongue at
Henry.

"And **DON'T YOU DARE** touch my
SNOWGIRL."

"I'll be watching you, Margaret."

"I'll be watching you, Henry."

They *glared* at each other.

Henry woke.

What was that noise? Was Margaret *sabotaging* his snowman? Was Susan *stealing* his snow?

Horrid Henry *dashed* to the window.

Phew. There was his ABOMINABLE SNOWMAN, big as ever, dwarfing every other snowman in the street. Henry's was definitely the **BIGGEST**, and the **BEST**. Umm boy, he could taste that **Triple Fudge Gooey Chocolate Chip Peanut Butter Marshmallow Custard ice cream** right now.

Horrid Henry climbed back into bed.

A tiny doubt nagged him.

Was his SNOWMAN definitely bigger than Margaret's?

'**course it was**, thought Henry.

"Are you sure?" rumbled his tummy.

"Yeah," said Henry.

"Because I really want that ice cream," growled his tummy. "Why don't you double-check?"

Horrid Henry got out of bed.

He was sure his was **BIGGER** and **BETTER** than Margaret's. He was

absolutely sure his was **BIGGER**
and **BETTER**.

But what if—

I can't sleep without checking,
thought Henry.

TIPTOE.

　TIPTOE.

　　TIPTOE.

Horrid Henry slipped out of the
front door.

The whole street was silent
and white and frosty. Every house
had a SNOWMAN in front. All of
them much smaller than Henry's, he

noted with satisfaction.

And there was his ABOMINABLE SNOWMAN looming up, Viking horns scraping the sky. Horrid Henry gazed at him proudly. Next to him was Peter's PATHETIC PIMPLE, with its stupid black stones. A SNOW LUMP, thought Henry.

Then he looked over at Margaret's **SNOWGIRL**. Maybe it had fallen down, thought Henry hopefully. And if it hadn't maybe he could help it on its way . . .

He looked again. And again. That *evil fiend!*

Margaret had sneaked an extra ball of snow on top, complete with a *huge flowery hat*.

That little

cheater, thought **Horrid Henry** indignantly. She'd *sneaked* out after bedtime and made hers bigger than his. How dare she? Well, he'd fix Margaret. He'd add more SNOW to his right away.

Horrid Henry looked around. Where could he find more SNOW? He'd already used up every drop on his front lawn to build his **GIANT**, and no new snow had fallen.

Henry shivered.

Brr, it was freezing. He needed more SNOW, and he needed it fast. His slippers were starting to feel very wet and cold.

Horrid Henry eyed Peter's pathetic lump of snow.

HMMM, thought Horrid Henry.

HMMM, thought Horrid Henry again.

Well, it's not doing any good sitting there, thought Henry. Someone could trip over it. Someone could hurt themselves. In fact, Peter's SNOW LUMP was a DANGER. He had to act fast before someone fell over it and broke a leg.

Quickly, he *scooped* up Peter's SNOWMAN and stacked it carefully on top of his. Then, standing on his TIPPY TOES, he balanced the Abominable Snowman's Viking horns on top.

DA DUM!

Much **BETTER**. And much **BIGGER** than Margaret's.

Teeth chattering, **Horrid Henry** sneaked back into his house and crept into bed. Ice cream, here I come, thought Horrid Henry.

DING DONG.

Horrid Henry **jumped** out of bed. What a morning to oversleep.

Perfect Peter ran and opened the door.

"We're from the **FROSTY FREEZE**
Ice Cream Factory," said the man,
beaming. "And you've got the winning
SNOWMAN out front."

"**I WON!**" screeched Horrid Henry.
"**I WON!**" He tore down the stairs
and out the door. Oh what a lovely
lovely day. The sky was blue. The sun
was shining — **huh???**

Horrid Henry looked around.

Horrid Henry's **ABOMINABLE**
SNOWMAN was gone.

"**MARGARET!**" screamed Henry.
"I'll kill you!"

But **MOODY MARGARET'S** SNOWGIRL
was gone, too.

The **ABOMINABLE SNOWMAN'S**
helmet lay on its side on the ground.
All that was left of Henry's snowman
was . . . Peter's PIMPLE, with its two
black stone eyes. A big blue ribbon was
pinned to the top.

"But that's **MY** snowman," said
Perfect Peter.

"**But . . . but . . .**" said Horrid Henry.

"You mean, I won?" said Peter.

"That's wonderful, Peter," said Mum.

"That's *fantastic*, Peter," said Dad.

"All the others melted," said the **FROSTY FREEZE** man. "Yours was the only one left. It must have been a **GIANT**."

"**It was**," howled Horrid Henry.

HORRID HENRY'S

BAKE-OFF

THWACK!
THWACK!
THWACK!

Moody Margaret thwacked
the wall with a stick.

Why oh why did she have to live
next door to someone as **HORRID** as
Henry?

Her club wasn't safe. Her biscuits
weren't safe. And he was such a
COPY-CAT. She'd told everyone she was
making a **chocolate** sponge cake for
the street party bake-off competition,

and now Henry was saying he was making a *chocolate* sponge cake. And pretending he'd thought of it first.

Well, she'd show him. Her cake was sure to 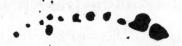 **WIN**. For once she'd have the last laugh.

Although . . .

Hmmm . . .

Maybe she could make sure of that . . .

A street party bake-off! Hurrah! **Horrid Henry** loved baking. What

could be better than choosing exactly
what you wanted to eat and then
cooking it exactly as you liked it?
With **LOADS** of extra sugar and
lashings of icing?

Horrid Henry loved making *fudge*.
Horrid Henry loved making *brownies*.
Horrid Henry loved baking *chocolate*
cakes.

His parents, unfortunately, only
liked him to make **HORRIBLE** food.
Pizzas ruined with vegetable toppings.
Sloppy **gloppy** porridge. And if they
ever let him make muffins, they

had to be wholesome muffins. With wholemeal flour. And bananas.

UGGGH.

But today, no one could stop him. It was a cake baking contest. And what a cake he'd make. His **chocolate** sponge cake with extra icing was guaranteed to win. He'd heard that copy-cat Margaret was making one too. Let old **FROG FACE** try. No one could out-bake Chef Henry.

Plus, the **WINNER** would get their picture in the paper AND be on TV, because the famous pastry chef

Cherry Berry
was coming
to judge.
Whoopee!

Everyone in
Henry's class
was taking
part.

Too bad, losers,
thought **Horrid Henry**,
dashing to the kitchen. Chef
Henry is in the room.

Unfortunately, someone else
was too.

Perfect Peter was wearing a Daffy Daisy apron and peering anxiously at the oven while Mum took out a baking tray laden with mysterious grey **globs**.

"Out of my way, *worm*," said Henry.

"I've made cupcakes for the bake-off," said Peter. "Look."

Perfect Peter proudly pointed to the plate covered in LUMPY blobs. His name was written on a flag poking out of one cupcake.

"Those aren't cupcakes," said Henry. "They're lopsided Cowpats."

"Mum," wailed Peter. "Henry called my cupcakes cowpats."

"Don't be **HORRID**, Henry," said Mum. "Peter, I think your cupcakes look — lovely."

"**PLOPCAKES** more like," said Henry.

"MUM!" screamed Peter. "Henry said plopcakes."

"Stop it, Henry," said Mum.

Tee hee.

All the better for him. No need to worry about Peter's SAGGY disasters winning.

His real competition was Margaret.

Henry hated to admit it, but she was almost as good a chef as he was. Well, no way was she beating him today. Her copy-cat **chocolate** sponge cake wouldn't be a patch on his.

"Henry. Peter. Come out and help hang up the bunting and get cloths on the tables," said Dad. "The street party starts at two o'clock."

"But I have to bake my cake," yelped Henry, weighing the *sugar* and **chocolate**. He always put in extra.

"There's plenty of time," said Mum. "But I need you to help me now."

MOODY MARGARET sneaked through the back door into Henry's kitchen. She'd waited until she'd seen Henry and his family go outside to help set up the tables.

If she was too late and his cake was already baking, she could open the oven door and **stomp** to make Henry's sponge COLLAPSE.

Or she could turn the temperature way up high, or *scoop* out the middle, or—

Margaret sniffed.

She couldn't smell anything baking.

What a bit of luck.

There were all Henry's ingredients on the counter, measured out and waiting to be used.

Snatch!

MOODY MARGARET grabbed the sugar jar and emptied it into the bin. Then she re-filled it with salt.

Tee hee, thought **MOODY MARGARET.**

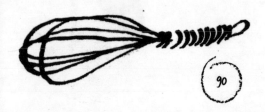

Wouldn't it be

wonderful to pay Henry back?

"What are you doing here?" came a little voice.

Oops.

MOODY MARGARET whirled round.

"What are you doing here?" said Margaret.

"I live here," said Peter.

"I must have come into the wrong house," said Margaret. "How silly of me."

"Out of my way, **worm**," came Henry's **HORRIBLE** voice as he slammed the front door.

"Byeeee," said Margaret, as she skedaddled out of the back door.

Phew.

Revenge was *sweet*, she thought happily. Or in this case, salty.

Should he tell Henry that Margaret had come over? No, thought Peter. Henry called my cupcakes **PLOPCAKES**.

Horrid Henry proudly stuck his name flag in his **FABULOUS** cake.

What a triumph.

His glorious **chocolate** sponge, drowning in ⓁⓊⓈⒸⒾⓄⓊⓈ icing, was definitely his best ever.

He was sure to win. He was absolutely sure to win. Just wait till *Cherry Berry* tried a mouthful of his cake. He'd be offered his own TV baking programme. He'd write his own cookbook. But instead of **HORRIBLE** recipes like 10 ways to cook broccoli — as if that would make any difference to how **YUCKY** it was — he'd have recipes for things kids actually liked to eat instead of what

93

their parents wanted them to eat.

Chips,

Chocolate worms,

FROSTY FREEZE ICE-CREAM,

VEG-FREE CHEESE PIZZA.

He'd write:

"Take wrapping off pizza. Put in oven. Or, if you are feeling lazy, ring Pizza Delivery to skip the boring unwrapping and putting in oven bit."

Yes! He'd add a few recipes with **ketchup**, then sit back and count the **DOUGH**.

Horrid Henry sighed happily. Didn't

that icing look **YUMMALICIOUS**.
He'd left loads in the bowl, and more
on the spoon. Oh boy, *chocolate*
here I come, thought Horrid Henry.
Chefs always taste their own food,
don't they, he thought, shoving a
huge succulent spoonful into his
mouth and—

BLECCCCCHHHHHH.
YUCK.

Horrid Henry gagged.

Ugh.

He spat it out, gasping and choking.

UGH.

It tasted worse than anything he'd ever tasted in his life. It was **HORRIBLE**. **Disgusting**. **Revolting**. Worse than sprouts.

So bitter. So salty.

Horrid Henry choked down some water.

How was it possible? What could he have done?

He'd been so careful, measuring out the ingredients. How could a teaspoon of salt have got into his icing?

But this wasn't even a TEASPOON.

This was a bucket load.

There was only one explanation . . .

Sabotage.

Peter must have done it, in revenge for Henry calling his cupcakes cowpats.

Wait till I get my hands on you, Peter, you'll be sorry, you *wormy worm toad*—

Wait.

Horrid Henry paused.

Was Perfect Peter evil enough to have come up with such a dastardly plan?

No.

Was he clever enough?

No.

It had to be someone so vile, so sly, so despicable, they would **sabotage** a cake.

There was only one person he knew who fitted that description.

MARGARET.

Well, he'd show her.

ROOT A TOOT!
ROOT A TOOT!
ROOT A TOOT TOOT TOOT!

Margaret was blasting away on her trumpet. Blasting what she thought was a victory tune.

Not this time, frog face, thought **Horrid Henry**, sneaking into MOODY MARGARET'S kitchen.

There was her **chocolate** sponge cake, resting proudly on a flowery china stand. What luck she'd copied him.

Whisk!

Henry snatched Margaret's cake.

Switch!

Henry plopped his salt cake on the cake stand instead.

Swap!

He stuck the name flag "Margaret" into his old cake.

Then he sneaked back home,
clutching his stolen one.

Horrid Henry placed his name flag
in Margaret's cake and stood back.

He had to admit, Margaret's cake
was GORGEOUS. So chocolatey.
So springy. So much *chocolate* icing
whirling and swirling in thick globs.

Margaret was a moody old grouch,
but she certainly knew how to bake
a cake.

It looked good enough to eat.

And then suddenly Horrid Henry had a **HORRIBLE** thought.

What if Margaret had baked a decoy cake, made with soap powder instead of flour, and left it out to tempt him to steal it? Margaret was so evil, it would be just like her to come up with such a cunning plan.

Don't let her fool you twice, screeched Henry's tummy.

He'd better take the TEENSIEST bite, just to make sure. He'd cover up the hole with icing, no problem.

Horrid Henry took a tiny bite

from the back.

Oh my.

Chocolate heaven.

This cake was great.

WOW.

But what if she'd put some bad bits in the middle? He'd better take another small bite just to check. He wouldn't want *Cherry Berry* to be poisoned, would he?

CHOMP
CHOMP
CHOMP

Horrid Henry stopped chewing.

Where had that **huge** hole in the cake come from? He couldn't have—

YIKES.

What was he thinking?

There was only one thing to do. He had to fill the hole fast. If he covered it with icing no one would ever know.

What could he fill the cake with to disguise the missing piece?

Newspaper?

Nah. Too bumpy.

Rice?

Too bitty.

Horrid Henry looked wildly around the kitchen.

Aha.

A SPONGE. A sponge for a sponge cake.

He was a genius.

Quickly Horrid Henry cut the sponge to fit the hole, slipped it inside and covered the joins with more icing.

Perfect.

No one would ever know.

Mum came into the kitchen.

"Hurry up, Henry, and bring your cake out. It's street party time."

Horrid Henry had a brilliant time at the street party. Everyone was there. Magic Martha did magic tricks in the corner. Jazzy Jim banged on his keyboard. Singing Soraya warbled behind the bouncy castle. Jolly Josh showed off his tap dancing.

Even Margaret playing solo
trumpet and Perfect Peter singing
with his band, The Golden Goodies,
couldn't ruin Henry's mood. He'd
eyed the other contestants as they
carried their entries to the bake-
off table. Rude Ralph had brought
burnt brownies. Sour Susan
had made **HORRIBLE** looking
gingerbread. Greedy Graham had
made a tottering tower of sweets
with **Chocolate Hairballs**, FOAM
TEETH, BELCHER-SQUELCHERS and
Blobby-Gobbers.

Then there were Peter's lopsided lumpies.

And Allergic Alice's gluten-free-nut-free-sugar-free-flour-free-dairy-free-beetroot-rice-cake.

Taste-free too, thought Horrid Henry.

And a rag-tag collection of DROOPY cakes and wobbly pies.

"Wah," wailed Weepy William. "I dropped mine."

Horrid Henry and MOODY MARGARET shoved through the crowd

as the famous judge, *Cherry Berry*, stood behind the cake table.

Henry had made sure his cake was at the front.

Margaret had also made sure her cake was at the front.

The two **chocolate** sponges faced each other.

"Nah nah ne nah nah, my cake is best," jeered Margaret.

"**Nah nah ne nah nah**, my cake is best," jeered Henry.

They *glared* at each other.

Tee hee, thought Margaret.

Tee hee, thought Henry.

"Stand back from the cakes, you'll all get a chance to taste them soon," said *Cherry Berry*.

She walked around the table, eyeing the goodies. She **poked** one, **prodded** another, sniffed a third. She walked around again. And again.

Then she stopped in front of Henry and Margaret's cakes.

Henry held his breath.

Yes!

"Now, don't these SPONGE cakes look lovely," said Cherry Berry. "So attractive. So fluffy. Ooh, I do love a light sponge," she said, cutting a piece and taking a big bite.

"So SPONGY," she choked, spitting out a piece of yellow kitchen sponge. "UGGGGHHH."

RATS, thought Horrid Henry.

Cherry Berry checked the name on the flag.

"Henry's cake is disqualified."

DOUBLE RATS, thought Horrid Henry.

"Ha ha ha ha ha," screeched Moody Margaret.

"The winner is . . . Margaret."

"**YES!**" shrieked Margaret.

Aaaarrrggghhhh.

That was his cake. It was so unfair. His cake had won after all. He'd pay Margaret back—

"I'll just try a little piece before we share it with everyone," said Cherry Berry, taking a huge bite.

"**BLECCCCHHH!**" gagged
Cherry, spitting it out. "Salt! Salt
instead of sugar."

"What?" screamed Moody Margaret.

How was it possible that salt had
been sneaked into her cake?

Unless . . . unless . . .

"You put a 𝕊ℙ𝕆ℕ𝔾𝔼 in my cake,"
shouted Margaret.

"You put salt in my cake," shouted
Henry.

Horrid Henry grabbed a pie and
hurled it at Margaret.

Moody Margaret grabbed a cake

and *hurled* it at Henry.

Horrid Henry **ducked**.

The **gooey** cake landed in *Cherry Berry's* face.

"Food fight!" shrieked Rude Ralph, snatching cupcakes and throwing them.

FOOD FIGHT!" screamed
Greedy Graham, pitching pies into the crowd.

"Stop it! Stop it!" shouted Mum, as whipped cream **splatted** on her head.

"Stop it!" shouted Dad, as a lemon tart **splatted** on his shirt.

Cherry Berry brushed cake from her face and pie from her hair.

"Wah," she wailed, as cake dripped down her back. "I have a soggy bottom."

She staggered over to the cake table and gripped the edge.

The table was empty except for a few grey cupcakes.

"I proclaim Peter's lopsided LUMPIES the winner," she gasped.

"Yippee," squealed Perfect Peter.

"Noooooo," howled Horrid Henry.

HORRID HENRY'S

CAR JOURNEY

"Henry! We're waiting!"

"Henry! Get down here!"

"Henry! I'm warning you!"

Horrid Henry sat on his bed and SCOWLED. His MEAN, horrible parents could warn him all they liked. He wasn't moving.

"HENRY! We're going to be late," yelled Mum.

"Good!" shouted Henry.

"HENRY! This is your final warning," yelled Dad.

"I DON'T WANT TO GO TO POLLY'S!" screamed Henry.

"I want to go to Ralph's birthday party."

Mum **stomped** upstairs.

"Well, you can't," said Mum. "You're coming to the christening, and that's that."

"**NO!**" screeched Henry. "I **HATE** Polly, I **HATE** babies, and I **HATE** you!"

Henry had been a pageboy at the wedding of his cousin, *Prissy Polly*, when she'd married PIMPLY PAUL. Now they had a *prissy*, PIMPLY baby, Vomiting Vera.

Henry had met Vera once before.

She'd thrown up all over him. Henry had hoped never to see her again until she was grown up and behind bars, but no such luck. He had to go and watch her be **dunked** in a vat of water, on the same day that Ralph was having a birthday party at **Goo-Shooter World**. Henry had been longing for ages to go to **Goo-Shooter World**. Today was his chance. His only chance. But no. Everything was **RUINED**.

Perfect Peter poked his head round the door.

"*I'm* all ready, Mum," said Perfect Peter. His shoes were polished, his teeth were **brushed**, and his hair neatly COMBED. "I know how annoying it is to be kept waiting when you're in a rush."

"Thank you, darling Peter," said Mum. "At least one of my children knows how to behave."

Horrid Henry ROARED and ~~ATTACKED~~. He was a *swooping* vulture digging his

122

claws into a dead MOUSE.

"AAAAAAAAAEEEEE!" squealed Peter.

"Stop being **horrid**, Henry!" said Mum.

"No one told me it was today!" screeched Henry.

"Yes we did," said Mum. "But you weren't paying attention."

"As usual," said Dad.

"*I knew we were going,*" said Peter.

"**I DON'T WANT TO GO TO POLLY'S!**"

screamed Henry. "I want to go to Ralph's!"

"Get in the car — **NOW**!" said Dad.

"Or no TV for a year!" said Mum.

ᴱᴱᴱᴷ! Horrid Henry stopped wailing. No TV for a year. Anything was better than that.

Grimly, he **stomped** down the stairs and out the front door. They wanted him in the car. They'd have him in the car.

"Don't **SLAM** the door," said Mum.

SLAM!

Horrid Henry *pushed* Peter away from the car door and scrambled for the right-hand side behind the driver. Perfect Peter **GRABBED** his legs and tried to climb over him.

VICTORY! Henry got there first.

Henry liked sitting on the right-hand side so he could watch the *speedometer*.

Peter liked sitting on the right-hand side so he could watch the *speedometer*.

"Mum," said Peter. "It's my turn to sit on the right!"

"No it isn't," said Henry. "It's mine."

"MINE!"

"**MINE!**"

"We haven't even left and already you're fighting?" said Dad.

"You'll take turns," said Mum. "You can swap after we stop."

Vroom. Vroom.

Dad started the car.

The doors locked.

Horrid Henry was trapped.

But wait. Was there a *glimmer* of hope? Was there a TEENY TINY chance? What was it Mum always said when he and Peter were *squabbling* in the car? "If you don't stop fighting I'm going to turn around and go home!" And wasn't home just exactly where he wanted to be? All he had to do was to do what he did best.

"Could I have a *story CD* please?"

said Perfect Peter.

"No! I want a **music CD**," said Horrid
Henry.

"I want 'Mouse Goes to Town'," said
Peter.

"I want '**Driller Cannibals'
Greatest Hits**'," said Henry.

"Story!"

"**Music!**"

"Story!"

"**Music!**"

SMACK!
SMACK!

"Waaaaaa!"

"Stop it, Henry," said Mum.

"Tell Peter to leave me alone!" screamed Henry.

"Tell Henry to leave me alone!" screamed Peter.

"Leave each other alone," said Mum.

Horrid Henry *glared* at Perfect Peter.

Perfect Peter *glared* at Horrid Henry.

Horrid Henry **stretched**. Slowly, steadily, centimetre by centimetre, he spread out into Peter's area.

"Henry's on my side!"

"No I'm not!"

"Henry, leave Peter alone," said Dad. "I mean it."

"I'm not doing anything," said Henry. "ARE WE THERE YET?"

"No," said Dad.

Thirty seconds passed.

"ARE WE THERE YET?" said Horrid Henry.

"No!" said Mum.

"ARE WE THERE YET?" said Horrid Henry.

"NO!" screamed Mum and Dad.

"We only left ten minutes ago,"
said Dad.

Ten minutes! Horrid Henry felt as if
they'd been travelling for hours.

"Are we a quarter of the way there
yet?"

"NO!"

"Are we halfway there yet?"

"NO!!"

"How much longer until we're halfway there?"

"STOP IT, HENRY!" screamed Mum.

"You're driving me **CRAZY!"** screamed Dad. "Now be quiet and leave us alone."

Henry sighed. Boy, was this boring. Why didn't they have a decent car, with BUILT-IN VIDEO GAMES, **MOVIES**, and a **jacuzzi?** That's just what he'd have, when he was king.

Softly, he started to HUM under his breath.

"Henry's HUMMING!"

"Stop being **horrid**, Henry!"

"I'm not doing anything," protested Henry. He lifted his foot.

"MUM!" squealed Peter. "Henry's **kicking** me."

"Are you **kicking** him, Henry?"

"Not yet," muttered Henry. Then he screamed. "MUM! PETER'S LOOKING OUT OF MY WINDOW!"

"Dad! Henry's looking out of *my* window."

"Peter *breathed* on me."

"Henry's *breathing* loud on purpose."

"Henry's **STARING** at me."

"Peter's on my side!"

"TELL HIM TO STOP!"

screamed Henry and Peter.

Mum's face was **RED**.

Dad's face was **RED**.

"THAT'S IT!" screamed Dad.

"I can't take this any more!" screamed Mum.

Yes! thought Henry. We're going to turn back!

But instead of turning round,

the car *screeched* to a halt at the
motorway services.

"We're going to take a break," said
Mum. She looked exhausted.

"Who needs a **wee**?" said Dad.
He looked even worse.

"Me," said Peter.

"Henry?"

"No," said Henry. He wasn't a baby. He

knew when he needed a **wee** and he didn't need one now.

"This is our only stop, Henry," said Mum. "I think you should go."

"**NO!**" screamed Henry. Several people looked up. "I'll wait in the car."

Mum and Dad were too tired to argue. They disappeared into the services with Peter.

RATS. Despite his best efforts, it looked like Mum and Dad were going to carry on. Well, if he couldn't make them turn back, maybe he could *delay* them? Somehow?

Suddenly Henry had a wonderful, SPECTACULAR idea. It couldn't be easier, and it was guaranteed to work. He'd miss the christening!

Mum, Dad, and Peter got back in the car. Mum drove off.

"I need a **wee**," said Henry.

"Not now, Henry."

"**I NEED A WEE!**" screamed Henry. "**NOW!**"

Mum headed back to the services.

Dad and Henry went to the toilets.

"I'll wait for you outside," said Dad. "Hurry up or we'll be late."

Late! What a lovely word.

Henry went into the toilet and locked the door. Then he **waited**. And **waited**. And **waited**.

Finally, he heard Dad's grumpy voice.

"Henry? Have you fallen in?"

Henry rattled the door.

"I'm locked in," said Henry. "The door's **STUCK**. I can't get out."

"Try, Henry," pleaded Dad.

"I have," said Henry. "I guess they'll have to break the door down."

That should take a few hours. He

settled himself on
the toilet seat and
got out a **COMIC**.

"Or you could just
crawl underneath
the partition into
the next stall," said Dad.

AAARGGHH. Henry could have **burst**
into tears. Wasn't it just his rotten
luck to try to get locked in a toilet
which had gaps on the sides? Henry
didn't much fancy *wriggling* round on
the cold floor. Sighing, he gave the
stall door a tug and opened it.

Horrid Henry sat in silence for the rest of the trip. He was so DEPRESSED he didn't even protest when Peter demanded his turn on the right. Plus, he felt **car sick**.

Henry rolled down his window.

"Mum!" said Peter. "I'm cold."

Dad turned the heat on.

"Having the heat on makes me feel **sick**," said Henry.

"I'm going to be **sick!**" whimpered Peter.

"I'm going to be **sick**," whined Henry.

"But we're almost there," screeched Mum. "Can't you hold on until—"

BLECCCHH.

Peter threw up all over Mum.

BLECCCHH.

Henry threw up all over Dad.

The car pulled into the driveway.

Mum and Dad st$_a$gg^{e}r$_e$d out of the car to Polly's front door.

"We survived," said Mum, mopping her dress.

"Thank God that's over," said Dad, mopping his shirt.

Horrid Henry **SCUFFED** his feet
sadly behind them. Despite all his
hard work, he'd lost the battle. While
Rude Ralph and Dizzy Dave and Jolly
Josh were *dashing* about
spraying each other
with **green goo**
later this afternoon,
he'd be stuck at a
boring party with
lots of grown-ups
YAK YAK YAKKING.
Oh misery!

DING DONG.

The door opened.

It was *Prissy Polly*.

She was in her bathrobe and slippers.

She carried a **STINKY**, smelly, wailing baby over her shoulder.

PIMPLY PAUL followed. He was wearing a **FILTHY** T-shirt with **sick** down the front.

"EEEEK," squeaked Polly.

Mum tried to look as if she had not been through **HELL** and barely lived to tell the tale.

"We're here!" said Mum brightly. "How's the lovely baby?"

"Too *prissy*," said Polly.

"Too PIMPLY," said Paul.

Polly and Paul looked at Mum and Dad.

"What are you doing here?" said Polly finally.

"We're here for the christening," said Mum.

"Vera's christening?" said Polly.

"It's *next* weekend," said Paul.

Mum looked like she wanted to

144

sag to the floor.

Dad looked like he wanted to sag beside her.

"We've come on the wrong day?" whispered Mum.

"You mean, we have to go and come back?" whispered Dad.

"Yes," said Polly.

"Oh no," said Mum.

"Oh no," said Dad.

"**BLECCCHH**," vomited Vera.

"EEEEK!" wailed Polly. "Gotta go."

She **slammed** the door.

"You mean, we can go home?" said

Henry. "Now?"

"Yes," whispered Mum.

"Whoopee!" screamed Henry. "Hang on, Ralph, here I come!"

HORRID HENRY'S

CHRISTMAS

Perfect Peter sat on the sofa looking through the **TOY HEAVEN** catalogue. Henry had **hogged** it all morning to write his Christmas present list. Naturally, this was not a list of the presents Henry planned to give. This was a list of what he wanted to get.

Horrid Henry looked up from his work. He'd got a bit **STUCK** after: a million pounds, a parrot, a machete, a swimming pool, a trampoline and a **KILLER CATAPULT**.

"Gimme that!" shouted Horrid

Henry. He **SNATCHED** the **TOY HEAVEN** catalogue from Perfect Peter.

"**YOU GIVE THAT BACK!**" shouted Peter.

"**IT'S MY TURN!**" shouted Henry.

"**YOU'VE HAD IT THE WHOLE MORNING!**" shrieked Peter. "Mum!"

"Stop being **HORRID**, Henry," said Mum, running in from the kitchen.

Henry ignored her. His eyes were glued to the catalogue. He'd found it. The toy of his dreams. The toy he had to have.

"I want a BOOM-BOOM BASHER," said Henry. It was a brilliant toy which CRASHED into everything, an ear-piercing siren wailing all the while. Plus all the trasher attachments. Just the thing for knocking down Perfect Peter's marble run.

"I've got to have a BOOM-BOOM BASHER," said Henry, adding it to his list in big letters.

"Absolutely not, Henry," said Mum. "I will not have that horrible noisy toy in my house."

"Aw, come on," said Henry. **"PLEEEASE."**

Dad came in.

"I want a **BOOM-BOOM BASHER** for Christmas," said Henry.

"No way," said Dad. "Too expensive."

"You are the *meanest*, most **HORRIBLE** parents in the whole world," screamed Henry. **"I HATE YOU!** I want a **BOOM-BOOM BASHER!"**

"That's no way to ask, Henry," said Perfect Peter. "I want doesn't get."

Henry *lunged* at Peter. He was an

octopus squeezing the life out of the helpless fish trapped in its tentacles.

"Help," SPLUTTERED Peter.

"Stop being **HORRID**, Henry, or I'll cancel the visit to Father Christmas," shouted Mum.

Henry stopped.

The smell of burning mince pies drifted into the room.

"Ahh, my pies!" shrieked Mum.

"How much longer are we going to have to wait?" whined Henry.

"I'm sick of this!"

Horrid Henry, Perfect Peter and Mum were standing near the end of a very long queue waiting to see Father Christmas. They had been waiting for a very long time.

"Oh, Henry, isn't this *exciting*," said Peter. "A chance to meet Father Christmas. I don't mind how long I wait."

"Well I do," **SNAPPED** Henry. He began to **squirm** his way through the crowd.

"Hey, stop **pushing!**" shouted Dizzy Dave.

"Wait your **TURN!**" shouted Moody Margaret.

"I was here **FIRST!**" shouted Lazy Linda.

Henry **SHOVED** his way in beside Rude Ralph.

"What are you asking Father Christmas for?" said Henry. "I want a **BOOM-BOOM BASHER**."

"Me too," said Ralph. "And a **Goo-Shooter**."

Henry's ears pricked up.

"What's that?'

"It's really cool," said Ralph. "It splatters green **goo** over everything and everybody."

"**YEAH!**" said Horrid Henry as Mum dragged him back to his former place in the queue.

"What do you want for Christmas, Graham?" asked Santa.

"Sweets!" said Greedy Graham.

"What do you want for Christmas, Bert?" asked Santa.

"I dunno," said Beefy Bert.

"What do you want for Christmas, Peter?" asked Santa.

"A dictionary!" said Peter. "Stamps, seeds, a geometry kit and some cello music, please."

"No toys?"

"No thank you," said Peter. "I have plenty of toys already. Here's a present for you, Santa," he added, holding out a beautifully wrapped

package. "I made it myself."

"What a delightful young man," said
Santa. Mum beamed proudly.

"My turn now," said Henry,
pushing Peter off Santa's lap.

"And what do you want for
Christmas, Henry?" asked Santa.

Henry unrolled the list.

"I want a BOOM-BOOM BASHER
and a **Goo-Shooter**," said Henry.

"Well, we'll see about that," said
Santa.

"**GREAT!**" said Henry. When grown-ups said "we'll see," that almost always meant "yes".

It was Christmas Eve.

Mum and Dad were *rushing* around the house tidying up as fast as they could.

Perfect Peter was watching a nature programme on TV.

"I want to watch **CARTOONS!**" said Henry. He *grabbed* the clicker and switched channels.

"I was watching the nature programme!" said Peter. "Mum!"

"Stop it, Henry," muttered Dad. "Now, both of you, help tidy up before your aunt and cousin arrive."

Perfect Peter jumped up to help. Horrid Henry didn't move.

"Do they have to come?" said Henry.

"Yes," said Mum.

"I **HATE** Cousin Steve," said Henry.

"No you don't," said Mum.

"I do too," SNARLED Henry. If there was a **YUCKIER** person walking

the earth than Stuck-Up Steve,
Henry had yet to meet him. It was
the one bad thing about Christmas,
having him come to stay every year.

DING DONG! It must be Rich
Aunt Ruby and his **HORRIBLE**
cousin. Henry watched as his aunt
STAGGERED in carrying boxes and
boxes of presents which she dropped

under the brightly lit tree. Most of them, no doubt, for Stuck-Up Steve.

"I wish we weren't here," moaned Stuck-Up Steve. "Our house is so much nicer."

"Shh," said Rich Aunt Ruby. She went off with Henry's parents.

Stuck-Up Steve looked down at Henry.

"Bet I'll get **LOADS** more presents than you," he said.

"Bet you won't," said Henry, trying to sound convinced.

"It's not what you get, it's the

thought that counts," said Perfect
Peter.

"*I'm* getting a BOOM-BOOM
BASHER and a **Goo-Shooter**," said
Stuck-Up Steve.

"So am I," said Henry.

"**NAH**," said Steve. "You'll just get
HORRIBLE presents like socks and
stuff. And won't I laugh."

When I'm king,
thought Henry, I'll
have a

SNAKE PIT made just for Steve.

"I'm *richer* than you," boasted Steve. "And I've got **loads more** toys." He looked at the Christmas tree.

"Call that TWIG a tree?" sneered Steve. "Ours is so **big** it touches the ceiling."

"Bedtime, boys," called Dad. "And remember, **NO ONE** is to open any presents until we've eaten lunch and gone for a walk."

"Good idea, Dad," said Perfect Peter. "It's always nice to have some *fresh air* on Christmas Day and leave the presents for later."

Ha, thought Horrid Henry. We'll see about that.

The house was dark. The only noise was the **rasping** sound of Stuck-Up Steve snoring away in his sleeping bag.

Horrid Henry could not sleep. Was there a BOOM-BOOM BASHER waiting for him downstairs?

He rolled over on his side and tried to get comfortable. It was no use.

How could he live until Christmas
morning?

Horrid Henry could bear it no
longer. He had to find out if he'd
been given a BOOM-BOOM BASHER.

Henry crept out of bed, *grabbed* his
torch, stepped over Stuck-Up Steve —
resisting the urge to stomp on him —
and sneaked down the stairs.

CR-EEAK went the creaky stair. Henry froze.

The house was silent.

Henry tiptoed into the dark sitting room. There was the tree. And there were all the presents, **LOADS** and **LOADS** and **LOADS** of them!

Right, thought Henry, I'll just have a quick look for my BOOM-BOOM BASHER and then get straight back to bed.

He seized a **GIANT** package. This looked promising. He gave it a shake. **THUD THUD THUNK**. This sounds good, thought Henry. His heart leapt. I just know it's a **BOOM-BOOM BASHER**. Then he checked the label: "Merry Christmas, Steve."

RATS, thought Henry.

He shook another temptingly shaped present: "Merry Christmas, Steve." And another: "Merry Christmas, Steve." And another. And another.

Then Henry felt a small, soft, **squishy** package. Socks for sure. I hope it's not for me, he thought. He checked the label:

"Merry Christmas, Henry."

There must be some mistake, thought Henry. Steve needs socks more than I do. In fact, I'd be doing him a favour giving them to him.

SWITCH! It was the work of a moment to swap labels.

Now, let's see, thought Henry. He eyed a **Goo-Shooter** shaped package with Steve's name on it, then found another, definitely book-shaped one, intended for himself. **SWITCH!**

Come to think of it, Steve had far too many toys cluttering up his house. Henry had heard Aunt Ruby complaining about the mess just tonight.

SWITCH! SWITCH! SWITCH! Then Horrid Henry crept back to bed.

It was 6:00 a.m.

"MERRY CHRISTMAS!"

shouted Henry. "Time to open the **presents!**"

Before anyone could stop him Henry **thundered** downstairs.

Stuck-Up Steve jumped up and followed him.

"**WAIT!**" shouted Mum.

"**WAIT!**" shouted Dad.

The boys *dashed* into the sitting room and flung themselves upon

the presents. The room was filled
with shrieks of delight and howls of
dismay as they tore off the wrapping
paper.

"Socks!" **SCREAMED** Stuck-Up Steve.
"What a crummy present! Thanks for
nothing!"

"Don't be so rude, Steve," said Rich
Aunt Ruby, yawning.

"A **Goo-Shooter!**" shouted Horrid
Henry. "**WOW!** Just what I wanted!"

"A geometry set," said Perfect Peter.
"Great!"

"A flower-growing kit?" howled

Stuck-Up Steve. "Phooey!"

"**MAKE YOUR OWN FIREWORKS!**" beamed Henry. "Wow!"

"Tangerines!" **SCREAMED** Stuck-Up Steve. "This is the **WORST** Christmas ever!"

"A **BOOM-BOOM BASHER!**" beamed Henry. "Gee, thanks. Just what I wanted!"

"Let me see that label," snarled Steve. He *grabbed* the torn wrapping paper. "Merry Christmas, Henry," read the label. There was no mistake.

173

"Where's my BOOM·BOOM BASHER?" SCREAMED Steve.

"It must be here somewhere," said Aunt Ruby.

"Ruby, you shouldn't have bought one for Henry," said Mum, frowning.

"I DIDN'T," said Ruby.

Mum looked at Dad.

"NOR ME," said Dad.

"Nor me," said Mum.

"FATHER CHRISTMAS gave it to me," said Horrid Henry. "I asked him to and he did."

Silence.

"HE'S GOT MY PRESENTS!"

SCREAMED Steve. "I want them back!"

"THEY'RE MINE!" SCREAMED

Henry, clutching his booty. "Father
Christmas gave them to me."

"NO, MINE!" SCREAMED

Steve.

Aunt Ruby inspected the labels.
Then she looked grimly at the two
howling boys.

"Perhaps I made a mistake when
I labelled some of the presents," she
MUTTERED to Mum. "Never mind. We'll sort

it out later," she said to Steve.

"IT'S NOT FAIR!" howled
Steve.

"Why don't you try on your new
socks?" said Horrid Henry.

Stuck-Up Steve *lunged* at Henry.
But Henry was ready for him.

"Aaaarggh!" screamed Steve, green goo dripping from his face and clothes and hair.

SPLAT!

"**HENRY!**" screamed Mum and Dad. "How could you be so *HORRID!*"

"**BOOM BOOM CRASH! NEE NAW NEE NAW WHOO WHOOO WHOOO!**"

What a great Christmas, thought Henry, as his **BOOM-BOOM BASHER** knocked over Peter's marble run.

"Say goodbye to Aunt Ruby, Henry," said Mum. She looked tired.

Rich Aunt Ruby and Steve had decided to leave a little earlier than planned.

"Goodbye, Aunt Ruby," said Henry.

"Goodbye, Steve. Can't **WAIT** to see you next Christmas."

"Actually," said Mum, "You're staying the night next month."

UH-OH, thought Horrid Henry.

HORRID HENRY'S

SLEEPOVER

**Horrid Henry loved
sleepovers. Midnight
feasts! Pillow fights!
Screaming and shouting!
Rampaging till dawn!**

The time he ate all the ice cream at
Greedy Graham's and left the freezer
door open! The time he jumped on all
the beds at Dizzy Dave's and **BROKE**
them all. And that time at Rude
Ralph's when he — well, hmmm,
perhaps better not mention that.

There was just one problem. No
one would ever have **Horrid Henry**

at their house
for a sleepover
more than once.
Whenever Henry
went to sleep at a
friend's house, Mum
and Dad were sure to get a
call at three o'clock from a demented
parent **SCREAMING** at them to pick up
Henry immediately.

Horrid Henry couldn't understand
it. Parents were so *fussy*. Even the
parents of great kids like Rude
Ralph and Greedy Graham. Who

cares about a LITTLE noise? Or a
BROKEN bed? **Big deal**, thought
Horrid Henry.

It was no **FUN** having friends
sleep over at *his* house. There was
no **RAMPAGING** and *feasting* at Henry's.
It was lights out as usual at nine
o'clock, no talking, no feasting,
NO FUN.

So when New Nick, who had just
joined Henry's class, invited Henry to
stay the night, Horrid Henry couldn't
believe his luck. New beds to **bounce**
on. New *biscuit* tins to raid. New

places to **RAMPAGE**. Bliss!

Henry packed his sleepover bag as fast as he could.

Mum came in. She looked GRUMPY.

"Got your pyjamas?" she asked.

Henry never needed pyjamas at sleepovers because he never went to bed.

"Got them," said Henry. Just not *with* him, he thought.

"Don't forget your toothbrush," said Mum.

"I won't," said **Horrid Henry**. He never *forgot* his toothbrush — he just chose not to bring it.

Dad came in. He looked even **GRUMPIER**.

"Don't forget your **COMB**," said Dad.

Horrid Henry looked at his **bulging** backpack stuffed with **TOYS** and **COMICS**. Sadly, there was no room for a **COMB**.

"I won't," lied Henry.

"I'm warning you, Henry," said Mum. "I want you to be on *best behaviour* tonight."

"Of course," said Horrid Henry.

"I don't want any phone calls at three o'clock from Nick's parents," said

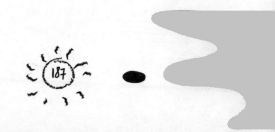

Dad. "If I do, this will be your last sleepover ever. I mean it."

Nag nag nag.

"All right," said Horrid Henry.

DING DONG.

WOOF WOOF WOOF WOOF WOOF!

A woman opened the door. She was wearing a **Viking helmet** on her head and long *flowing* robes. Behind her stood a man in a velvet cloak holding

back five **ENORMOUS**, **SNARLING** black dogs.

"TRA LA LA BOOM-DY AY," boomed a dreadful, ear-splitting voice.

"**BRAVO, BRAVO!**" shouted a chorus from the sitting room.

GRRRRRRR! growled the dogs.

Horrid Henry hesitated. Did he have the right house? Was New Nick an **alien?**

"Oh don't mind us, dear, it's our opera club's karaoke night," trilled the Viking Helmet.

"Nick!" bellowed the Cloak. "Your friend is here."

Nick appeared. Henry was glad to see he was **NOT** wearing a Viking helmet or a velvet cloak.

"Hi, Henry," said New Nick.

"Hi, Nick," said Horrid Henry.

A little girl toddled over, sucking her thumb.

"Henry, this is my sister, Lily," said Nick.

Lily *gazed* at **Horrid Henry**.

"I love you, Henwy," said Lisping Lily. "Will you marry with me?"

"NO!" said **Horrid Henry**.

Uggh. What a **REVOLTING** thought.

"Go away, Lily," said Nick.

Lily did not move.

"Come on, Nick, let's get out of here," said Henry. No **TODDLER** was going to spoil *his* fun. Now, what would he do first, **RAID** the kitchen, or **bounce** on the beds?

"Let's **RAID** the kitchen," said Henry.

"Great," said Nick.

"Got any good sweets?" asked Henry.

"Loads!" said New Nick.

Yeah! thought **Horrid Henry**. His sleepover FUN was beginning!

They sneaked into the kitchen. The floor was covered with dog blankets, overturned food bowls, clumps of DOG HAIR and gnawed dog bones. There were a few suspicious-looking PUDDLES. Henry hoped they were water.

"Here are the biscuits," said Nick.

Henry looked. Were those DOG HAIRS all over the jar?

"Uh, no thanks," said Henry. "How about some sweets?"

"Sure," said Nick. "Help yourself."

He handed Henry a bar of chocolate. YUMMY! Henry was about to take a BIG BITE when he stopped. Were those — teeth marks in the corner?

"Raaa!" A big black shape jumped on Henry, knocked him down and snatched the chocolate.

Nick's dad burst in.

"Rigoletto! Give that back!" said Nick's dad, *yanking* the chocolate out of the dog's mouth.

"Sorry about that, Henry," he said, offering it back to Henry.

"Uhh, maybe later," said Henry.

"Okay," said Nick's dad, putting the **slobbery** chocolate back in the cupboard.

Eeew, gross, thought Horrid Henry.

"I love you, Henwy," came a lisping voice behind him.

"AH HA HA HA HA HA HA HA!"

warbled a high, piercing voice from
the sitting room.

Henry held his ears. Would the
windows shatter?

"**Encore!**" shrieked the opera
karaoke club.

"Will you marry with me?" asked
Lisping Lily.

"Let's get out of here," said **Horrid
Henry**.

Horrid Henry *leapt* on Nick's bed.

Yippee, thought Horrid Henry.

Time to get bouncing.

BOUNCE—
Crash!

The bed collapsed in a heap.

"What happened?" said Henry.
"I hardly did anything."

"Oh, I **BROKE** the bed ages ago,"
said Nick. "Dad said he was tired
of fixing it."

RATS, thought Henry. What a lazy
dad.

"How about a pillow fight?" said
Henry.

"No pillows," said Nick. "The dogs chewed them."

Hmmn.

They *could* sneak down and RAID the freezer, but for some reason Henry didn't really want to go back into that kitchen.

"I know!" said Henry. "Let's watch TV."

"Sure," said New Nick.

"Where is the TV?" said Henry.

"In the sitting room," said Nick.

"But — the KARAOKE," said Henry.

"Oh, they won't mind," said Nick. "They're used to noise in this house."

"DUM DUM DE DUM DUMM
DUMM DUM DE DUM DUMM
DUMM!"

Horrid Henry sat with his face
pressed to the TV. He couldn't
hear a word **Mutant Max** was
shrieking with all that racket in the
background.

"Maybe
we should
go to bed,"
said Horrid
Henry,
sighing.

Anything to get away from the noise.

"Okay," said New Nick.

Phew, thought Horrid Henry.
Peace at last.

SNORE! SNORE!

Horrid Henry turned over in
his sleeping bag and tried to get
comfortable. He **HATED** sleeping
on the floor. He **HATED** sleeping
with the window open. He **HATED**
sleeping with the radio on. And he
HATED sleeping in the same room as

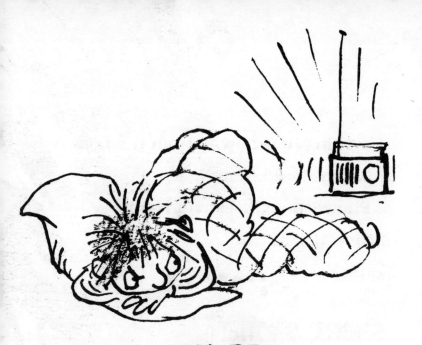

someone who **SNoRED**.

AWHOOOOOOO! howled the winter
wind through the open window.
SNORE! SNORE!

"I'M JUST A LONESOME COWBOY, LOOKIN' FOR A
LONESOME COWGIRL," blared the radio.

WOOF WOOF WOOF barked the dogs.

"**Yeowwww!**"
squealed Henry,
as five **wet**,
smelly dogs
pounced
on him.

"AWHOOOOOOO!"
howled the
wind.

SNORE! SNORE!

"TOREADOR — on guard!"
boomed the opera karaoke
downstairs.

Horrid Henry loved noise. But

this was *too much*.

He'd have to find somewhere else
to sleep.

Horrid Henry *flung* open the
bedroom door.

"I love you, Henwy," said Lisping
Lily.

Slam! Horrid Henry shut the
bedroom door.

Horrid Henry did not *move*.

Horrid Henry did not BREATHE.

Then he opened
the door a
fraction.

"Will you marry with me, Henwy?"

AAARRRGH!!!

Horrid Henry ran from the bedroom and **barricaded** himself in the linen cupboard. He settled down on a pile of towels.

Phew. Safe at last.

"I want to give you a big kiss, Henwy," came a little voice beside him.

NOOOOOOO!

It was three o'clock.

"TRA LA LA BOOM-DY AY!"

"—LONESOME COWBOY!"

SNORE! SNORE!

AWHOOOOOOOOOOOOO!

WOOF! WOOF! WOOF!

Horrid Henry crept to the hall phone and dialled his number.

Dad answered.

"I'm so sorry about Henry, do you want us to come and get him?" Dad mumbled.

"Yes," wailed Horrid Henry. "I need my rest!"

HORRID HENRY

GOES SHOPPING

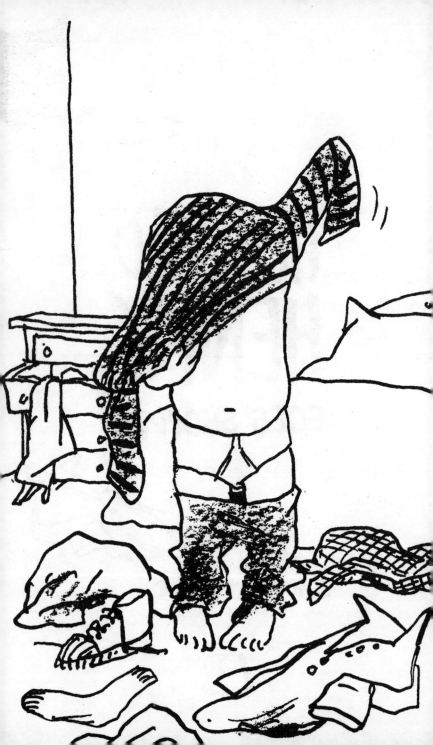

Horrid Henry stood in his bedroom up to his knees in clothes. The long-sleeve stripy T-shirt came to his elbow. His trousers stopped halfway down his legs. Henry sucked in his tummy as hard as he could. Still the zip wouldn't zip.

"Nothing fits!" he screamed, YANKING off the shirt and HURLING it across the room. "And my shoes hurt."

"All right, Henry, calm down," said Mum. "You've grown. We'll go out this afternoon and get you some new clothes and shoes."

"**NOOOOOOO!**" shrieked Henry. "**NOOOOOOOOOOOOO!**"

Horrid Henry **HATED** shopping.

Correction: Horrid Henry **LOVED** shopping. He **LOVED** shopping for gigantic TVs, *computer games*, COMICS, *toys* and sweets. Yet for some reason Horrid Henry's parents never wanted to go shopping for good stuff. Oh no. They shopped for Hoover bags. Toothpaste. Spinach. Socks. Why oh why did he have such

HORRIBLE parents? When he was
a grown-up he'd never set foot in
a supermarket. He'd only shop for
TVs, *computer games* and chocolate.

But shopping for clothes was even
worse than heaving his **HEAVY BONES**
round the HAPPY SHOPPER
Supermarket. Nothing was more
boring than being *dragged* round

miles and miles and miles of shops, filled with **disgusting** clothes only a **MUTANT** would ever want to wear, and then standing in a little room while Mum made you try on ICKY SCRATCHY things you wouldn't be seen dead in if they were the last trousers on earth. It was **horrible** enough getting dressed once a day without doing it fifty times. Just thinking about trying on shirt after shirt after shirt made Horrid Henry want to scream.

"I'M NOT GOING SHOPPING!" he howled, kicking the pile of clothes

as viciously as he
could. "And you
can't make me."

"What's all
this yelling?"
demanded Dad.

"Henry needs new trousers," said
Mum grimly.

Dad went pale.

"Are you sure?"

"Yes," said Mum. "Take a look
at him."

Dad looked at Henry. Henry
SCOWLED.

"They're a little small, but not that
bad," said Dad.

"I can't **breathe** in these trousers!"
shrieked Henry.

"That's why we're going shopping,"
said Mum. "And I'll take him." Last
time Dad had taken Henry shopping
for socks and came back instead
with three Hairy Hellhound CDs and
a jumbo pack of **Day-Glo slime**.

"I don't know what came over me,"
Dad had said, when Mum told
him off.

"But why do I have to go?" said

Henry. "I don't want to waste my precious time shopping."

"What about my precious time?" said Mum.

Henry SCOWLED. Parents didn't have precious time. They were there to serve their children. New trousers should just magically appear, like clean clothes and packed lunches.

Mum's face brightened. "Wait, I have an idea," she *beamed*. She rushed out and came back with a large plastic bag. "Here," she said, pulling out a pair of **BRIGHT RED**

TROUSERS, "try
these on."

Henry looked at
them suspiciously.

"Where are they
from?"

"Aunt Ruby dropped
off some of Steve's old clothes a
few weeks ago. I'm sure we'll find
something that fits you."

Horrid Henry *stared* at Mum. Had
she gone GAGA? Was she actually
suggesting that he should wear his
horrible cousin's mouldy old shirts

and pongy pants? Just imagine
putting his arms into the same
STINKY sleeves that Stuck-Up Steve
had **slimed**? Uggh!

"**NO WAY!**" screamed Henry,
shuddering. "I'm not wearing Steve's
smelly old clothes. I'd catch rabies."

"They're practically brand new,"
said Mum.

"I don't care," said Henry.

"But Henry," said Perfect Peter,
"I always wear your **HAND-ME-DOWNS**."

"So?" snarled Henry.

"I don't mind wearing **HAND-ME-**

DOWNS," said Perfect Peter. "It saves so much money. You shouldn't be so **selfish**, Henry."

"Quite right, Peter," said Mum, smiling. "At least one of my sons thinks about others."

Horrid Henry *pounced*. He was a *vampire* sampling his supper.

"*AAIIIEEEEEE!*" squealed Peter.

"Stop that, Henry!" screamed Mum.

"Leave your brother alone!"
screamed Dad.

Horrid Henry glared at Peter.

"Peter is a **worm**, Peter is a **toad**,"
jeered Henry.

"Mum!" wailed Peter. "Henry said I
was a **worm**. And a **toad**."

"Don't be **HORRID**, Henry," said Dad.
"Or no **TV** for a week. You have
three choices. Wear Steve's old
clothes. Wear your old clothes. Go
shopping for new ones today."

"Do we have to go today?" moaned
Henry.

"Fine," said Mum. "We'll go
tomorrow."

"I don't want to go tomorrow," wailed
Henry. "My weekend will be ruined."

Mum *glared* at Henry.

"Then we'll go right now this minute."

"**NO!**" screamed Horrid Henry.

"YES!" screamed Mum.

Several hours later, Mum and
Henry walked into **MELLOW MALL**.
Mum already looked like she'd been

crossing the **Sahara desert** without water for days. Serve her right for bringing  me here, thought **Horrid Henry**, scowling, as he scuffed his feet. "Can't we go to 𝕊ℍ𝕆ℙ 'ℕ' 𝔻ℝ𝕆ℙ?" whined Henry. "Graham says they've got a win-your-weight-in-chocolate competition."

"No," said Mum, *dragging* Henry into *Zippy's Department Store*. "We're here

to get you some new trousers and
shoes. Now hurry up, we don't have
all day."

Horrid Henry looked around.
WOW! There was lots of great stuff
on display.

"I want the **Hip-Hop Robots**," said
Henry.

"No," said Mum.

"I want the new **Supersoaker!**"
screeched Henry.

"No," said Mum.

"I want a **Creepy Crawly** lunchbox!"
"**NO!**" said Mum, pulling him into

the boys' clothing department.

What, thought **Horrid Henry** grimly, is the point of going shopping if you never buy anything?

"I want **ROOT-A-TOOT** trainers with flashing red lights," said Henry. He

could see himself
now, strolling
into class, a
bugle blasting

and red light flashing every time his
feet hit the floor. COOL! He'd love to
see Miss Battle-Axe's face when he
exploded into class wearing them.

"No," said Mum, shuddering.

"Oh please," said Henry.

"NO!" said Mum. "We're here to buy
trousers and sensible school shoes."

"But I want ROOT-A-TOOT trainers!"
screamed Horrid Henry. "Why can't

we buy what I want to buy? You're the **MEANEST** mother in the world and I hate you!"

"Don't be **horrid**, Henry. Go and try these on," said Mum, *grabbing* a selection of **hideous** trousers and **revolting** T-shirts. "I'll keep looking."

Horrid Henry sighed loudly and slumped towards the dressing room. No one in the world suffered as much as he did. Maybe he could hide between the clothes racks and never come out.

Then something **WONDERFUL** in

the toy department next door caught his eye.

Whooa! A whole row of the new *megalotronic animobotic robots* with 213 programmable actions. Horrid Henry dumped the clothes and ran over to have a look. Oooh, the new Intergalactic Samurai Gorillas which launched real *stinkbombs!* And the latest **Supersoakers!**

And deluxe **Dungeon Drink** kits with a celebrity chef recipe book! To say nothing of the **MEGA-WHIRL GOO SHOOTER** which sprayed **fluorescent goo** for fifty metres in every direction. **WOW!**

Mum staggered into the dressing room with more clothes. "Henry?" said Mum.

No reply.

"**HENRY!**" said Mum.

Still no reply.

Mum *yanked* open a dressing room door.

227

"Hen—"

"EXCUSE ME!" yelped a bald man, standing in his underpants.

"Sorry," said Mum, blushing bright pink. She dashed out of the changing room and scanned the shop floor.

Henry was gone.

Mum searched *up* the aisles.

No Henry.

Mum searched *down* the aisles.

Still no Henry.

Then Mum saw a tuft of hair sticking up behind the neon sign for **BALLISTIC BAZOOKA BOOMERANGS**. She marched over and hauled Henry away.

"I was just looking," protested Henry.

Henry tried on one pair of trousers after another.

"**NO, NO, NO, NO, NO, NO, NO**," said Henry, kicking off the final pair. "I hate all of them."

"All right," said Mum, grimly. "We'll look somewhere else."

Mum and Henry went to TOP TROUSERS. They went to *Cool Clothes*. They went to **Stomp in the Swamp**. Nothing had been right.

"Too tight," moaned Henry.

"Too itchy!"

"Too big!"

"Too small!"

"Too ugly!"

"Too red!"

"**TOO UNCOMFORTABLE!**"

"We're going to *Tip-Top Togs*," said Mum wearily. "The first thing that fits, we're buying."

Mum staggered into the children's department and grabbed a pair of

pink and green tartan trousers in Henry's size.

"Try these on," she ordered. "If they fit we're having them."

Horrid Henry *gazed* in horror at the horrendous trousers.

"Those are girls' trousers!" he screamed.

"They are not," said Mum.

"**ARE TOO!**" shrieked Henry.

"I'm sick and tired of your excuses, Henry," said Mum. "Put them on or no pocket money for a year. I mean it."

Horrid Henry put on the **pink and green tartan trousers**, puffing out his stomach as much as possible. Not even Mum would make him buy trousers that were TOO TIGHT.

Oh no. The **HORRIBLE** trousers had an elastic waist. They would fit a mouse as easily as an **ELEPHANT**.

"And lots of room to grow," said Mum brightly. "You can wear them for years. Perfect."

"**NOOOOOO!**" howled Henry. He flung himself on the floor kicking and screaming.

"NOOOO! THEY'RE GIRLS' TROUSERS!!!"

"We're buying them," said Mum. She gathered up the **tartan trousers** and stomped over to the till. She tried not to think about starting all over again trying to find a pair of shoes that Henry would wear.

A little girl in pigtails walked out of the dressing room, twirling in

pink and green tartan trousers.

"I love them, Mummy!" she shrieked. "Let's get three pairs."

Horrid Henry stopped howling.

He looked at Mum.

Mum looked at Henry.

Then they both looked at the **pink and green tartan trousers** Mum was carrying.

ROOT-A-TOOT!
ROOT-A-TOOT!
ROOT-A-TOOT!
TOOT! TOOT!

An earsplitting bugle blast shook the house. Flashing red lights **bounced** off the walls.

"What's that noise?" said Dad, covering his ears.

"What noise?" said Mum, pretending to read.

ROOT-A-TOOT!
ROOT-A-TOOT!
ROOT-A-TOOT!
TOOT! TOOT!

Dad *stared* at Mum.

"You didn't," said Dad. "Not —
ROOT-A-TOOT trainers?"

Mum hid her face in her
hands.

"I don't know what came
over me," said Mum.

HORRID HENRY'S

EXTRA HORRID GUIDE TO PERFECT PARENTS

Shhh. Shhh. Are you
alone? Is anyone
watching you read this?
Spies are everywhere.
Find a private place where
your parents and brothers
and sisters can't see you .
. .

Okay, good. Then I'll begin.

My first guide to Perfect
Parents was too popular. And too
DANGEROUS. Parents bought
all the copies and hid them. They
knew once my Purple Hand Gang

got hold of my **TOP TIPS** for parent control they'd never be the boss again.

But I couldn't let all that **fantastic**, *amazing* advice go to waste.

So. Here's my plan.

Inside this book I've copied down all the best bits from my Parent Taming manual. And then I've added even more **FANTASTIC** advice. Study my extra **HORRID** guide and perfect parents can be yours. My **TOP TIPS** will teach you everything you need to know about training your parents. After all, who's the boss? You? Or them?

Too right, you. And don't let them forget it. It's hard, heavy work training perfect parents, but do it right and it will be worth it.

Remember, hide this book from prying eyes, including tell-tale little brothers and sisters. It's your **SECRET WEAPON**.

No Parents Allowed

And oh yeah. I know you'll thank me for ever, but words are cheap. All donations gratefully received.

Perfect Parents let you do whatever you want, whenever you want. They let you decide what's for dinner, never make you eat **vegetables** and give you control of the **TV** remote. They always blame your brothers and sisters whenever there's

a quarrel. But how, I hear you **SCREAM**, can you turn your **meAn, HORRIBLE, BOSSY** parents into perfect ones? Just follow my simple training tips. It's all about Discipline, Rewards, Consistency and Limits.

Shame and Tame

Remind your parents daily how *marvellous* your friends' parents are. Sigh **LOUDLY** and say, "I wish I had Ralph's parents. They always let

him stay up late/eat as many sweets as he wants/watch loads of TV etc." Other great phrases to shame and tame parents: "Margaret's parents gave her a **Demon Dagger Sabre**"; "Josh's parents let him pour his own **chocolate** sauce"; "Gurinder's parents give loads more pocket money than you"; "Susan's parents let her

play on the computer for as long as she likes".

Telling them how **WONDERFUL** other parents are will make them want to shape up fast.

make parents feel guilty

Believe it or not, most parents try their best. Shame their best is so bad. But that's why it's a cinch to make your parents feel guilty.

Try using any of the phrases below. Once you make them feel guilty, then give them a chance to feel better by giving you what you want.

"You must feel **TERRIBLE** being such a bad parent."

"Ralph's mum is much nicer than you."

"Everyone else gets more **POCKET MONEY** than I do."

"Margaret doesn't have a *sweet* day."

"You're the **WORST** dad in the world and I hate you."

Note. The last phrase is a bit **extreme** and only for use in dire emergencies.

Praise good behaviour

No one likes being told off all the time. Even parents. So remember, gang, when they give you those extra sweets you deserve, or let you watch extra TV, PRAISE their good behaviour. You want to make them do this all the time. Parents want praise and attention, so give it to them. Trust me, they'll be rushing to stuff extra DESSERTS into you, and letting you off your chores.

Speaking of chores . . .

How to make your parents do your chores for_you

What are you, **A BUTLER?** How dare parents ask you to help around the house. Don't you have enough to do as it is?

Have you ever heard that phrase, "If you want something done well, do it yourself?" Parents

know this is true, so your goal is to do all chores so slowly, and so badly, and so ungraciously, and with so much *wailing* and **GNASHING** and **GROANING** and MOANING and SIGHING, that your parents will give up and yell: "Oh, all right, I'll do it myself."

VICTORY!

Congratulations. You are now well on your way to having perfectly trained parents.

Tantrums

All parents have tantrums. They **YELL**

and **SCREAM** when they don't get their way (i.e. when you don't do what they want). Just remember, you'd have tantrums too if you were old and wrinkly like them. My advice is, keep cool. Suggest your parent has a time-out. If you are really an expert parent tamer, urge them to sit on the **NAUGHTY** step until they calm down.

Of course, tantrums are your secret weapon. Tantrums are

best staged in public, or just before your parents have to go somewhere important, or when guests are over. Believe me, they'll promise you anything if you'll only just **STOP** screaming.

Best Tantrum Positions

Face down on the floor is best. This means you can **kick** and SQUEAL, and make lots of extra noise. Plus, if you are fake crying, it's much easier to do this when your parents can only hear and not see you.

Money

You want it. They have it. **IT'S SO unfair**. Why do parents have so much more money than you do? Wouldn't it be great if you could have all the **CASH**, and give them pocket money? Well, when I'm *King,* that's exactly what will happen. Till then, you just have to try and get as much money as you can by making your

parents feel guilty.

Tell them everyone gets **LOADS** more pocket money than you do.

Remind them of all the things you need to buy.

Point out that they can't expect any presents from you if they give you so little money.

Tell them you need to practise *money management skills* and you can't on the pitiful amount they give you.

If all else fails . . . tell them it's time for a raise.

Sadly, there are always things that you want that for some reason parents don't want you to have. For example, **ROLLER BOWLERS**, the world's best trainers, the shoes on wheels you can set to *Screech*, **FIRE-ENGINE**, *Drums*, **Cannon**, SIREN and **Sonic Boom**. They're so loud you can hear them from miles off! **WOW!** So, how do you make them buy you great stuff like that? You **BORE** and *NAG* them to death. Just go on and on and on about them.

Believe me, they will eventually give in just to keep you quiet. Then don't forget, **PRAISE GOOD BEHAVIOUR**. You want to reinforce this excellent conduct and help your parents make good choices.

That way, next time you won't have to **WHINE** quite so much.

How to get the food you want

Just one word — **allergies**. I know I'm **allergic** to fruit, vegetables, soup, salad and muesli. In fact, the

only foods I can eat are **CHOCOLATE**, cake, **crisps**, BURGERS, *pizza* and SWEETS.

How to get your siblings into trouble

Why should you take the rap? Divert your parents' attention on to the guilty — your **annoying** brothers and sisters. Remember. **You're** always right. **They're** always wrong.

Unfortunately, parents don't always see things clearly. They might blame you, even though it's never your fault.

Here's how to train your parents to see things your way.

Make sure you start **YELLING** first. Don't wait to be accused of **STEALING** your brother's chips. Loudly accuse him of **STEALING/HITTING/PINCHING/TEASING** etc.

"He/she started it" is your go-to phrase.

But remember.

There's one skill you **MUST** learn. *Crying on command.* Whatever happens, your parents must find you in tears. Trust me, screeching "He hit me," or "She pinched me," while *wailing* and **GNASHING** and **gulping** and sobbing will carry so much more weight, even if (GASP) you were the one who started the fight.

Your younger brothers and sisters already know this fact. That's why they use pretend crying all the time.

Just because you're older, don't forget this invaluable tip.

When in doubt – **CRY**.

When you're in the wrong – **CRY**.

When you've teased them – **CRY**.

Get your tears in first.

Weasel Words

Remember my favourite charity,
CHILD IN NEED? The one I collect
money for?

That's a perfect example of *weasel
words*. I'm a child. I'm in need. **100%
TOTALLY TRUE**. Can I help it if whoever
gives me money gets the wrong idea?
Tee hee.

Weasel words can come to your rescue in TIGHT spots.

"I didn't touch his sweets." (I ate them.)

"Dad said I could." (Well, he did — once.)

"Peter hit me!" (He did, once, when he was a baby. I didn't say when he did . . .)

"I've only watched an hour of **TV**." (The TV was on for hours but I wasn't watching it.)

When all else fails, **DENY EVERYTHING**. You have no idea how those biscuits ended up in your room.

TV

Remember the **magic word**? No, it's not **please**, it's homework. You'd be amazed how much **TV** you can watch by saying it's for homework. Parents like to feel they're helping their children in school, so what better way to help than to let kids watch *"educational"* programmes like **Terminator Gladiator**,

Mutant Max and **Hog House** (tee hee).

Bedtime

Always tricky. Parents want you in bed as early as possible. You, of course, want to stay up as late as possible. So if your bedtime is **8 o'CLOCK**, here are some parent-training tips to get that **EXTRA** time you deserve. One is sure to work.

1. Tell them **EVERYONE** gets to stay up later than you do.
2. Delay bedtime for as long as

possible. See how slowly you can brush your teeth. *Drag* your feet as you **s**t**a**g**g**e**r** up the stairs to your bedroom. Take hours putting on your pyjamas. Say you need to do your homework. Ask for endless **drinks of water**. Once in bed, keep coming downstairs. Any excuse will do.

3. Once you have **TORMENTED** them sufficiently, promise that if they let you stay up an hour later, you'll go to bed with no fuss. (Then keep your

word, and your parents will learn that they can spend an hour **struggling** to heave you into bed at **8 O'CLOCK**, or have a quiet evening with no fuss and stress and argument. The *well-trained* parent will make the right choice.)

Congratulations

WELL DONE! You are now the proud owner of *perfectly trained and tamed*

parents. You
call the shots,
as you lounge
around eating
chocolates
and guzzling
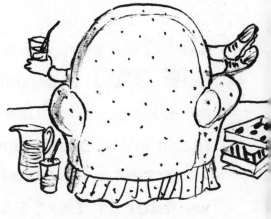
FIZZYWIZZ drinks while your
perfect parents wait on you hand
and foot, eager to do whatever—

Wait, what's that you're saying?
You did everything I told you, and
they aren't tamed? Then they must
have read this book and armed
themselves against all your **weasel**

words. I did warn you, this information is **TOP SECRET**, how could you let your parents get hold of this book, now they'll know exactly how to—

Come to think of it, I wonder if that's why my parents seem to be resisting their training . . .

oops.

HORRID
HENRY
STEALS THE
SHOW

"How many badges do you have, Henry?" asked Perfect Peter.

"Tons," said **Horrid Henry**. "Now out of my way, worm, I'm busy." He'd just got hold of the latest **SKELETON SKUNK AND THE WIZARD OF WONDER** story and was desperately trying to finish it before Dad started **NAGGING** him to do his homework.

"I already have ten badges," said Perfect Peter. "That's five more than I need to go on the school trip to **WILD WATER-SLIDE PARK**."

"Bully for you," said Horrid Henry.

"You know that tomorrow is the deadline to earn all your badges," said Peter.

Horrid Henry stopped reading. WHAT? **WHAT?**

That was **IMPOSSIBLE**.

He had weeks and weeks and weeks left to get those *stupid* badges. Hadn't he already signed up to do the sound effects for Miss Battle-Axe's dreadful school play, *THE GOOD FOOD FAIRY*, just so he could earn his Entertainer badge?

And now he had to earn **FOUR** more? **BY TOMORROW?**

272

It was so unfair.

But there was no time to lose if he wanted to race down the **ZOOM OF DOOM**, the most **TERRIFYING** water slide in the universe, or **Belly Flop Drop**, or all the other **BRILLIANT**, *amazing*, **FANTASTIC** rides at the best water-slide rollercoaster park in the **WHOLE WIDE WORLD**. Horrid Henry had always wanted to go. But his mean, **horrible** parents would never take him.

Horrid Henry pushed past Peter, dashed to his bedroom and grabbed the Badge Sheet he'd been given ages ago from under a pile of **DIRTY SOCKS** and **MUDDY JEANS**. Frantically, he skimmed it, searching for the *quickest*, **easiest** badges to earn.

Why did so many badges involve hard work? Ugh. Where was the **TV-WATCHING BADGE** when he needed it?

Horrid Henry scanned the list. Let's see, let's see — *Take Care of an Animal* badge. He took care of **FAT** 𝓕𝓵𝓾𝓯𝓯𝔂, didn't he, by letting him sleep all the time. Oh wait. *Look after an animal for two months.* Henry didn't have two months, he had one night.

Hiking badge? No way. Horrid Henry **SHUDDERED**. Too dangerous. **RAMPAGING CHICKENS**, **MARAUDING VAMPIRES** — who knew what horrible monsters were waiting just to nab him as he *heaved* his heavy bones?

What a shame he'd been disqualified from earning the *Giving Good Advice* badge after *Vain Violet* had asked: *"How can I be more beautiful?"* and Henry had replied, **"change your head."**

Wait. Wait.

A *Cooking* badge.

YES YES YES!

"I'm cooking tonight," shouted Horrid Henry.

"I'm cooking tonight," said Perfect Peter. "I want to get another badge . . ."

Horrid Henry marched into Peter's

bedroom, grabbed Peter's favourite sheep, Fluff Puff, and DANGLED it over the loo.

"Who's cooking tonight?" said **Horrid Henry**.

"You are," wailed Peter.

Mum stared at the pile of **CRISPS** on her plate.

Dad stared at the pile of **CRISPS** on his plate.

Peter stared at the pile of **CRISPS** on his plate.

"Eat up," said Horrid Henry, stuffing **CRISPS** into his mouth. "There's seconds."

"Why are we eating **CRISPS** for dinner?" said Dad.

"It's the first course of your two-course meal so I can earn my *Cooking* badge," said Henry. "I have to include two vegetables. **OVEN CHIPS** with **Ketchup** coming up."

"This is **NOT** healthy eating," said Mum.

"Is too," said Horrid Henry. "**Ketchup** is a vegetable, which is

278

why it's called **tomato** ketchup. **CHIPS**
and **CRISPS** are made from potatoes.
And I've already done the different
ways to prepare and cook food part."

Hadn't he *ordered* a pizza this
month? *Tick*. **Microwaved**
a burger? *Tick*. And *taken the wrapper
off* a chocolate bar? *Tick tick tick.*
That *Cooking* badge was his.

Dad ate a handful of **CRISPS** and
then patted his stomach. "I shouldn't
really, I need to banish my belly,"
he said. "All my trousers are getting
tight."

"So stop eating, **fatso**," said Horrid
Henry.

"Don't be **horrid**, Henry!" said
Mum.

"I'm not being **horrid**," said Henry.
"I'm earning my *Handy Helper* badge
by helping Dad banish his belly. So
please can you sign my form? About
how considerate and caring I am?"

"**NO**," said Mum.

"**NO**," said Dad.

"**ARRRRGGGGHHH!**" wailed Horrid
Henry. "I need the badges **NOW**."

"*You have to earn badges*," said *Perfect Peter*.

"Quite right, Peter," said Mum.

Horrid Henry scowled. Here he was, working his **guts** off to earn badges, and his **MEAN**, **horrible** parents were being **MEAN** and **horrible**.

And as for his *wormy worm* brother . . .

"Mum, Dad, listen to the song I wrote," said Henry. "It's for my **Write and Sing a Song** badge."

Horrid Henry leapt on to a chair and started to sing.

"PETER IS A **POOP POOP POOPSICLE.**
NO ONE IS A **WORMIER WORM.**
HE'S A **NINNY** AND A **MINI**
SHOULD BE THROWN INTO A **BIN-i,**
HE'S A **POOP POOP POOP POOP POOPSICLE.**"

"Mum!" wailed Peter. "Henry called me a poopsicle."

"That's a ~~TERRIBLE~~ song, Henry," said Dad.

"No it isn't," said Henry. "It rhymes. And I wrote it myself. Where does it say it has to be a *nice* song?"

"Henry . . ." said Mum.

"Oh all right," said Horrid Henry.

"I'll sing one more."

If only there was a **PARENT SWAP** badge

. . .

"HENRY IS THE TOP
HENRY IS THE BEST.
YOU DON'T EVEN NEED
TO PUT IT TO THE TEST.

MARGARET IS A FROG-FACE
SHE'S A DISGRACE.
I WISH SHE'D BLAST OFF

INTO OUTER SPACE —
NO! HYPER-SPACE!
THEN I'D NEVER HAVE TO SEE
THAT FROGGY FROGGY
FROG-FACE AGAIN.
RIBBIT."

Dad signed for the **Write and Sing a Song** badge.

Mum signed for the *Cooking* badge.

Dad signed for the *Handy Helper* badge but only on condition that Henry set and cleared the table for a month.

Three badges down. The fourth, the **Entertainer** badge, would be his tomorrow. Then, just one more to get.

The **COLLECTOR** badge! Of course. Didn't he collect gizmos? And comics? Yes he did.

TICK.

There was one last requirement to get that badge. *Talk about someone else's collection.*

"**I hate your sheep collection, Peter!**" bellowed **Horrid Henry.**

TICK.

He'd earned the *Cooking* badge, the *Handy Helper* badge, the **Write and Sing a Song** badge and the **COLLECTOR** badge.

Just one more badge and it's WATERPARK, HERE I COME, thought

Henry. All he had to do was do the sound effects for **MISS BATTLE-AXE'S TERRIBLE** play tomorrow, and he'd be *whizzing* down the **ZOOM OF DOOM** in no time.

Horrid Henry sat backstage with the soundboard on a table in front of him. All the buttons were labelled:

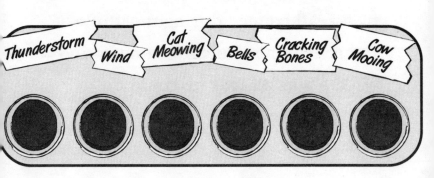

Thunderstorm Wind Cat Meowing Bells Cracking Bones Cow Mooing

The second row sounds were:

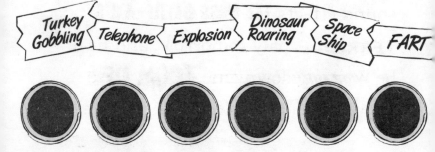

Turkey Gobbling Telephone Explosion Dinosaur Roaring Space Ship FART

"DO NOT TOUCH the second row," hissed **MISS BATTLE-AXE**. "Every sound you need for this play is in the **TOP ROW**. Do exactly what we rehearsed."

Horrid Henry scowled. Naturally, he'd read comics during most of the rehearsals, but providing sound effects was *so easy* he could do it

in his sleep.

MISS BATTLE-AXE walked on to the stage.

"Welcome, everyone, to our class play, *THE GOOD FOOD FAIRY*, written by me. I'm also delighted to welcome the theatre critic from our local paper. We look forward to his review of our show."

The auditorium lights dimmed. **SOUR SUSAN** appeared, dressed in black.

"*IT WAS A DARK AND STORMY NIGHT*," said Susan. Henry pressed the **THUNDERSTORM** button.

BANG! BANG! BANG! BOOM! BOOM! BOOM!

"THE WIND WAS HOWLING —" Horrid Henry pressed the *Wind* button — *Whooooooooooo* — "and snow was falling on poor, hungry Tiny Tim."

Brainy Brian sat cross-legged on stage, holding a crutch and shivering, as **ANXIOUS ANDREW** emptied a bucket of paper snow on him.

"What a **TERRIBLE** Victorian night," said Tiny Tim. "I wonder what's for supper? Wouldn't it be great to have a nice **plump** roast turkey? Oh no! **GRUEL** again! How I wish I had some fresh food like broccoli to eat. Or string beans, or tomatoes, or apples. If only I could travel to the future and enjoy a healthy meal.

"But hark! What's that I hear? It

must be the *Good Food Fairy*, coming to visit."

Ding-a-ling! Ding-a-ling. Henry chimed the fairy bells as Moody Margaret swept on to the stage.

"Hello, poor person from the past," said Margaret. She waved her wand. "I've come to grant your wish. Let me show you the *wonderful* food of the future.

"First, drink *milk* and eat **cheese** for strong bones. You don't want your bones to break—"

CRUNCH CRACK

CRUNCH CRACK

"—because you haven't eaten enough calcium."

Margaret the *Good Food Fairy* continued **YAKKING** about different food groups to poor bored Tiny Tim. And the poor bored audience.

"A balanced diet is made up of the five food groups," she lectured.

"1. Protein.

2. Fruit and vegetables . . ."

Horrid Henry *yawned*. He could see the theatre critic asleep in the front row. Better wake him up, thought

Henry. After all, the storm must still be going on.

Horrid Henry pressed the Thunderstorm button.

BANG BANG BANG BOOM BOOM BOOM

The critic woke up and *scribbled* furiously in his notebook.

The Good Food Fairy droned on.

Horrid Henry felt his eyelids droop. What a **DULL** play. If only he, Henry, had written this play, it would have been so much more exciting. He'd have had **TERMINATOR GLADIATOR** challenge the *Good Food Fairy* to a duel for a start, then—

"Sound effect!" *hissed* Miss Battle-Axe.

YIKES, thought Horrid Henry. Which sound effect?

Horrid Henry had no idea. He *jabbed* at the sound board.

The audience laughed.

MOOOOOOOO!

OOPS. Hadn't they met the cow yet? He vaguely remembered that Tiny Tim tripped over a cow at some point.

"**I SAID,** THE GOOD FOOD FAIRY HAS LANDED ON HER DAINTY FEET," yelled Margaret, as the ear-splitting *MOOing* continued.

Horrid Henry quickly took his finger off the *Moo* button.

Dainty feet. Dainty feet? Didn't someone break a foot because they hadn't eaten enough calcium?

Horrid Henry pressed the Cracking Bones button.

CRUNCH! CRACK! CRUNCH! CRACK!

"Who's coming with us to the future?" shouted the *Good Food Fairy*, trying to be heard over the sound of breaking bones. "Why, it's Mr Vitamin! Hello, Mr Vitamin."

Weepy William crept on to the stage. He looked terrified.

There was a

TERRIBLE silence.

"**SOUND EFFECT!**" *hissed* Miss Battle-Axe again.

Mr Vitamin? Who on earth was Mr Vitamin? thought Henry. Was he a **turkey**? There was a **turkey** in the play somewhere. Henry was sure someone had said **turkey**. He pressed the button.

Gobble gobble gobble,

gobble gobble gobble.

"I said, 'Hello, Mr Vitamin',"
repeated Margaret, glaring.

**Gobble gobble gobble,
gobble gobble gobble.**

"MR VITAMIN," screeched
Margaret. "Tiny Tim's *CAT*."

Cat? thought Henry. Boring! He
should be a **DINOSAUR.** This stupid
play would be so much better if he
were a **DINOSAUR.**

Horrid Henry pressed the button.

ROARRRRRRRR!

Weepy William opened his mouth
and then closed it. He'd obviously
forgotten his line.

Better help him, thought Horrid
Henry.

RING RING. RING RING.

"That's a Victorian phone," shouted
Henry from the wings. "Why don't
you answer it, Mr Vitamin?"

William didn't move.

VROOM! VROOM! VROOM! VROOM!

"Look, it's a spaceship, Mr Vitamin," shouted Henry. "Hop aboard."

"Waaaaaaaaaa," wailed Weepy William.

"I forgot my line."

"And now I must leave you," yelled the **Good Food Fairy**.

"But before I go I must—"

A terrible fart noise blasted out.

The audience howled.

Horrid Henry beamed. After all, someone had to save the show.

Horrid Henry skipped home. He'd done it! Miss Battle-Axe had refused to give him his **Entertainer** badge until she read the critic's review the next day, which ended:

"The sound effects stole the show, turning what could have been a tedious play into a comedy tour de force. I hope we see many future performances of THE GOOD FOOD FAIRY."

HORRID HENRY'S

CHRISTMAS PRESENTS

23 December
(just two more days
to go!!!)

Horrid Henry sat by the
Christmas tree and stuffed himself
full of the special sweets he'd nicked
from the special Christmas Day
stash when Mum and Dad weren't
looking. After his triumph in the
school Christmas play, Horrid
Henry was feeling delighted with
himself and with the world.

Granny and Grandpa, his grown-up

cousins PIMPLY PAUL and PRISSY POLLY, and their baby Vomiting Vera were coming to spend Christmas.

WHOOPEE, thought Horrid Henry, because they'd all have to bring him presents. Thankfully, Rich Aunt Ruby and STUCK-UP STEVE weren't coming. They were off skiing. Henry hadn't forgotten the DREADFUL LIME-GREEN CARDIGAN Aunt Ruby had given him last year. And much as he hated his cousin POLLY, anyone was better than STUCK-UP STEVE, even someone who squealed all the time and had a baby who *threw up* on everyone.

Mum *dashed* into the sitting room, wearing a flour-covered apron and looking frantic. Henry choked down his mouthful of *sweets*.

"Right, who wants to decorate the tree?" said Mum. She held out a cardboard box brimming with *tinsel* and gold and silver and blue *baubles*.

"**Me!**" said Henry.

"*Me!*" said Peter.

Horrid Henry *dashed* to the box and **scooped** up as many shiny ornaments as he could.

"I want to put on the gold baubles," said Henry.

"I want to put on the *tinsel*," said Peter.

"Keep away from my side of the tree," hissed Henry.

"You don't have a side," said Peter.

"Do too."

"Do not," said Peter.

"I want to put on the *tinsel* **and** the baubles," said Henry.

"But I want to do the **tinsel**," said Peter.

"**Tough**," said Henry, draping Peter in **tinsel**.

"Muuum!" wailed Peter. "Henry's **HOGGING** all the decorations! And he's putting **tinsel** on me."

"Don't be **HORRID**, Henry," said Mum. "Share with your brother."

Peter carefully wrapped blue **tinsel** round the lower branches.

"Don't put it there," said Henry, *yanking* it off. Trust Peter to ruin his beautiful plan.

311

"MUUUM!" wailed Peter.

"HE'S WRECKING MY DESIGN,"

screeched Henry. "He doesn't know how to decorate a tree."

"But I wanted it there!" protested Peter. "Leave my *tinsel* alone."

"You leave **my stuff** alone then," said Henry.

"HE'S WRECKED MY DESIGN!" shrieked Henry and Peter.

"Stop **FIGHTING**, both of you!" shrieked Mum.

"He started it!" screamed Henry.

"Did not!"

"Did too!"

"That's enough," said Mum. "Now, whose turn is it to put the fairy on top?"

"I don't want to have that **STUPID** fairy," wailed Horrid Henry. "I want to have **Terminator Gladiator** instead."

"No," said Peter. "I want the fairy. We've always had the fairy."

"Terminator!"

"Fairy!"

TERMINATOR!"

"Fairy!"

SLAP!

SLAP!

"WAAAAAAA!"

"We're having the fairy," said Mum
firmly, "and I'll put it on the tree."

"**NOOOOO!**" screamed Henry.
"Why can't we do what I want to do?
I never get to have what I want."

"Liar!" whimpered Peter.

"I've had enough of this," said Mum. "Now get your presents and put them under the tree."

Peter *ran* off.

Henry stood still.

"Henry," said Mum. "Have you finished wrapping your Christmas presents?"

Yikes, thought Horrid Henry. What am I going to do now? The moment he'd been **DREADING** for weeks had arrived.

"Henry! I'm not going to ask
you again," said Mum. "Have you
finished wrapping all your Christmas
presents?"

"**Yes!**" bellowed Horrid Henry.

This was not entirely true. Henry
had not finished wrapping his
Christmas presents. In fact, he
hadn't even started. The truth
was, Henry had finished wrapping
because he had **NO PRESENTS** to wrap.

This was certainly not his fault.
He had bought a few gifts, certainly.
He knew Peter would have loved the

box of green **Day-Glo slime**. And if
he didn't, well, he knew who to give
it to. And Granny and Grandpa and
Mum and Dad and Paul and Polly
would have adored the **big boxes**
of chocolates Henry had won at the
school fair. Could he help it if the
chocolates had called his name so
loudly that he'd been **forced** to eat
them all? And then Granny had
been complaining about gaining
weight. Surely it would have been
very unkind to give her chocolate.
And eating chocolate would have just

317

made PIMPLY PAUL'S PIMPLES worse. Henry'd done him a big favour eating that box.

And it was hardly Henry's fault when he'd needed extra for a raid on the SECRET CLUB and Peter's present was the only stuff to hand. He'd meant to buy replacements. But he had so many things he needed to buy for himself that when he opened his skeleton bank to get out some cash for Christmas shopping, only 35p had rolled out.

"I've bought and wrapped all my presents,

Mum," said Perfect Peter. "I've been saving my pocket money for months."

"**WHOOPEE** for you," said Henry.

"Henry, it's always better to give than to receive," said Peter.

Mum *beamed*. "Quite right, Peter."

"Says who?" growled Horrid Henry. "I'd much rather get presents."

"Don't be so **HORRID**, Henry," said Mum.

"Don't be so selfish, Henry," said Dad.

Horrid Henry stuck out his tongue. Mum and Dad gasped.

"You **HORRID** boy," said Mum.

"I just hope *Father Christmas* didn't see that," said Dad.

"Henry," said Peter, "*Father Christmas* won't bring you any presents if you're **bad**."

AAARRRGGHHH! Horrid Henry *sprang* at Peter. He was a GRIZZLY BEAR guzzling a **juicy morsel**.

"AAAAIIEEE," wailed Peter. "Henry pinched me."

"**HENRY! GO TO YOUR ROOM**," said Mum.

"**FINE!**" screamed Horrid Henry, **stomping** off and *slamming* the door. Why did he get stuck with the world's **meanest** and most **HORRIBLE** parents? They certainly didn't deserve any presents.

Presents! Why couldn't he just *get* them? Why oh why did he have to *give* them? Giving other people presents was such a waste of his

hard-earned money. Every time he
gave a present it meant something
he couldn't buy for himself. Goodbye
chocolate. Goodbye COMICS. Goodbye
DELUXE GOO-SHOOTER. And then,
if you bought anything good, it was
so HORRIBLE having to give it away.
He'd practically cried having to give
Ralph that Terminator Gladiator poster
for his birthday. And the Mutant
Max lunchbox Mum made him give
Kasim still made him gnash his teeth
whenever he saw Kasim with it.

Now he was stuck, the night before

322

Christmas Eve, with **NO MONEY**, and **NO PRESENTS** to give anyone, deserving or not.

And then Henry had a wonderful, **SPECTACULAR** idea. It was so wonderful, and so **SPECTACULAR**, that he couldn't believe he hadn't thought of it before. Who said he had to *buy* presents? Didn't Mum and Dad always say it was the thought that counted? And oh boy was he thinking.

Granny was sure to love a **Mutant Max** comic. After all, who wouldn't? Then when she'd finished enjoying

323

it, he could borrow it back. **Horrid Henry** rummaged under his bed and found a recent copy. In fact, it would be a shame if Grandpa got jealous of Granny's great present. Safer to give them each one, thought Henry, digging deep into his pile to find one with the fewest torn pages.

Now let's see, Mum and Dad. He could draw them a lovely picture. Nah, that would take too long. Even better, he could write them a poem.

Henry sat down at his desk, grabbed a pencil and wrote:

Dear Old baldy Dad
Don't be sad
Be glad
Because you've had...
A very merry Christmas
Love from your Lad,
Henry

Not bad, thought Henry. Not bad.
And **SO CHEAP!** Now one for Mum.

Dear Old wrinkly Mum
Don't be glum
Cause you've got a fat tum
And an even bigger bum
Ho ho ho hum
Love from your son,
Henry

WOW! It was hard finding so many

words to rhyme with "mum" but he'd

326

done it. And the poem was nice and Christmassy with the "**HO HO HO**". "Son" didn't rhyme but hopefully Mum wouldn't notice because she'd be so thrilled with the rest of the poem. When he was *famous* she'd be proud to show off the poem her son had written specially for her.

Now, **POLLY**. Hmmmn. She was always SQUEAKING and SQUEALING about dirt and dust. Maybe a lovely kitchen sponge? Or a rag she could use to mop up after **VERA**? Or a bucket to put over PIMPLY PAUL'S head?

Wait. What about some **SOAP?**

Horrid Henry nipped into the bathroom. Yes! There was a tempting bar of blue **SOAP** going to waste in the soap dish by the bathtub. True, it had been used once or twice, but a bit of smoothing with his fingers would sort that out. In fact, POLLY and PAUL could share this present, it was such a good one.

Whistling, Horrid Henry wrapped up the soap in sparkling reindeer paper. He was a *genius*. Why hadn't he ever done this before? And a lovely

328

rag from under the sink would be perfect as a gag for **Vera**.

That just left **Peter** and all his present problems would be over. A piece of **chewing gum**, only one careful owner? A collage of *sweet wrappers* which spelled out **Worm**? The unused comb Peter had given him last **Christmas**?

Aha. Peter loved *bunnies*. What better present than a picture of a *bunny*?

It was the work of a few moments for Henry to draw a *bunny* and slash

Henry

a few blue lines across it to colour it in. Then he signed his name in **big letters** at the bottom. Maybe he should be a *famous artist* and not a poet when he grew up, he thought, admiring his handiwork. Henry had heard that artists got paid **LOADS OF CASH** just for stacking a few bricks or *hurling* paint at a white canvas. Being an artist sounded like a great job, since it left so much time for

playing computer games.

Horrid Henry dumped his
presents beneath the Christmas tree
and sighed happily. This was one
Christmas where he was sure to get
a lot more than he gave. **WHOOPEE!**
who could ask for anything
more?

HORRID HENRY'S

AMBUSH

Christmas Eve
(Just a few more hours to go!)

It was Christmas Eve at last. Every minute felt like an hour. Every hour felt like a year. How could Henry live until Christmas morning when he could get his hands on all his **LOOT?**

Mum and Dad were **baking** frantically in the kitchen.

Perfect Peter sat by the twinkling Christmas tree scratching out

"Silent Night" over and over again on his cello.

"Can't you play something else?" snapped Henry.

"No," said Peter, sawing away. "This is the only Christmas Carol I know. You can move if you don't like it."

"You move," said Henry.

Peter ignored him.

"Siiiiiiiilent Niiiiight," screeched the cello.

AAARRRGH.

Horrid Henry lay on the sofa with his fingers in his ears, double-checking his choices from the **TOY HEAVEN** catalogue. Big red "**X**"s appeared on every page, to help you-know-who remember all the toys he absolutely had to have. Oh **please**, let everything he wanted leap from its pages and into *Santa's* sack. After all, what could be better than looking at a **huge,** glittering stack of presents on Christmas morning, and knowing that they were all for you?

Oh **please** let this be the year when he **finally** got everything he wanted!

His letter to *Father Christmas* couldn't have been clearer.

Dear Father Christmas,

I want loads and loads and loads of cash, to make up for the puny amount you put in my stocking last year. And a Robomatic Supersonic Space Howler Deluxe plus attachments would be great, too. I have asked for this before, you know!!! And the Terminator Gladiator fighting kit. I need lots more Day-Glo slime and comics and a Mutant Max poster and the new Zapatron Hip-Hop Dinosaur. This is your last chance.

Henry

PS Satsumas are NOT presents!!!!!

PPS Peter asked me to tell you to give me all his presents as he doesn't want any.

How hard could it be for *Father Christmas* to get this right? He'd asked for the **Space Howler** last year, and it never arrived. Instead, Henry got . . . vests. And handkerchiefs. And books. And clothes. And a — **BLEUCCCCK** — jigsaw puzzle and a skipping rope and a **tiny supersoaker** instead of the **mega-sized** one he'd specified. **Yuck!**

Father Christmas obviously needed Henry's help.

Father Christmas is getting old and doddery, thought Henry. Maybe he hasn't got my letters. Maybe he's lost his reading glasses. Or — what a **HORRIBLE** thought — maybe he was delivering Henry's presents by mistake to some other **Henry**. **EEEEK!** Some **yucky**, undeserving Henry was probably right now this minute playing with

Henry's **Terminator Gladiator** sword, shield, axe and trident. And enjoying his **Intergalactic Samurai Gorillas**. It was so unfair!

And then suddenly Henry had a brilliant, **SPECTACULAR** idea. Why had he never thought of this before? All his present problems would be over. Presents were far too important to leave to *Father Christmas*. Since he couldn't be trusted to bring the right gifts, **Horrid Henry** had no choice. He would have to **AMBUSH** *Father Christmas*.

Yes!

He'd hold *Father Christmas* hostage with his **Goo-Shooter** while he rummaged in his present sack for all the loot he was owed. Maybe Henry would keep the lot. Now that would be fair.

Let's see, thought Horrid Henry. *Father Christmas* was bound to be a *slippery* character, so he'd need to **BOOBY-TRAP** his bedroom. When you-know-who sneaked in to fill his stocking at the end of the bed, Henry could *leap up* and nab him. *Father*

Christmas had a lot of explaining to do for all those years of stockings filled with satsumas and walnuts instead of chocolate and **COLD HARD CASH**.

So, how best to capture him?

Henry considered.

A bucket of water above the door.

A skipping rope stretched tight across the entrance, guaranteed to **trip up** intruders.

A web of STRING criss-crossed from bedpost to door and threaded with bells to **ENSNARE** night-time visitors.

And let's not forget strategically
scattered WHOOPEE cushions.

His plan was foolproof.

Loot, here I come, thought Horrid Henry.

Horrid Henry sat up in bed, his **Goo-Shooter** aimed at the half-open door where a bucket of water balanced. All his *traps* were laid. No one was getting in without Henry knowing about it. Any minute now, he'd catch *Father Christmas* and make him pay up.

Henry **WAITED**. And **WAITED**. And **WAITED**. His eyes started to feel heavy and he closed them for a moment.

There was a rustling at Henry's door.

Oh my god, this was it! Henry lay down and pretended to be asleep.

CR-EEEEAK.
CR-EEEEAK.

Horrid Henry reached for his **Goo-Shooter**.

A **huge** shape loomed in the doorway.

Henry braced himself to attack.

"Doesn't he look *sweet* when he's asleep?" whispered the shape.

"What a little *snugglechops*," whispered another.

Sweet? Snugglechops?

Horrid Henry's fingers itched

to let Mum and Dad have it with both barrels.

Henry could see it now. Mum covered in green **goo**. Dad covered in green **goo**. Mum and Dad snatching the **Goo-Shooter** and wrecking all his plans and *throwing* out all his presents and banning him from **TV** for ever . . . hmmmn. His fingers felt a little less itchy.

Henry lowered his **Goo-Shooter**. The bucket of water **WOBBLED** above the door.

Yikes! What if Mum and Dad

stepped into his *Santa* traps? All his hard work — ruined.

"I'm awake," snarled Henry.

The shapes stepped back. The water stopped WOBBLING.

"Go to sleep!" hissed Mum.

"GO TO SLEEP!" hissed Dad.

"What are you doing here?" demanded Henry.

"Checking on you," said Mum. "Now go to sleep or *Father Christmas* will never come."

He'd better, thought Henry.

Horrid Henry woke with a jolt. **AAARRGGH!** He'd fallen asleep. How could he? **Panting** and *gasping,* Henry switched on the light. **PHEW.** His traps were intact. His stocking was empty. *Father Christmas* hadn't been yet.

WOW, WAS THAT LUCKY. That was incredibly lucky. Henry lay back, his heart pounding.

And then Horrid Henry had a **TERRIBLE** thought.

What if *Father Christmas* had decided to be **spiteful** and avoid

Henry's bedroom this year? Or what if he'd played a sneaky trick on Henry and filled a stocking downstairs instead?

Nah. No way.

But wait. When *Father Christmas* came to Rude Ralph's house he always filled the stockings downstairs. Now Henry came to think of it, Moody Margaret always left her stocking downstairs too, hanging from the fireplace, not from the end of her bed, like Henry did.

Horrid Henry looked at the clock.

It was past midnight. Mum and Dad had forbidden him to go downstairs till morning, on pain of having all his presents taken away and no TELLY all day.

But this was an **EMERGENCY**. He'd creep downstairs, take a quick peek to make sure he hadn't missed *Father Christmas*, then be back in bed in a jiffy.

No one will ever know, thought Horrid Henry.

Henry TIPTOED round the WHOOPEE cushions, leaped over the criss-cross

threads, stepped over the skipping rope and carefully squeezed through his door so as not to disturb the bucket of water. Then he crept downstairs.

Sneak
   Sneak
      Sneak

Horrid Henry shone his torch over the sitting room. *Father Christmas* hadn't been. The room was exactly as he'd left it that evening.

Except for one thing. Henry's

light illuminated the Christmas tree, heavy with *chocolate* santas and *chocolate* bells and *chocolate* reindeer. Mum and Dad must have hung them on the tree after he'd gone to bed.

Horrid Henry looked at the *chocolates* cluttering up the Christmas tree. Shame, thought **Horrid Henry**, the way those chocolates **SPOIL** the view of all those lovely decorations. You could barely see the baubles and *tinsel* he and Peter had worked so hard to

354

put on.

"Hi, Henry,"
said the *chocolate*
santas. "Don't you want to
eat us?"

"Go on, Henry," said the *chocolate*
bells. "You know you want to."

"What are you waiting for, Henry?"
urged the *chocolate* reindeer.

What indeed? After all, it was
Christmas.

Henry took a *chocolate* santa
or three from the side, and then
another two from the back. Hmmn,

boy, was that great chocolate, he thought, stuffing them into his mouth.

Oops. Now the chocolate santas looked a little unbalanced.

Better take a few from the front and from the other side, to even it up, thought Henry. Then no one will notice there are a few chocolates missing.

Henry **gobbled** and **GORGED** and guzzled. WOW, WERE THOSE CHOCOLATES YUMMY!!!

The tree looks a bit bare, thought

Henry a little while later.
Mum had such eagle eyes
she might notice that a
few — well, all — of the
chocolates were missing.
He'd better hide all
those gaps with a few extra
baubles. And, while he was improving
the tree, he could swap that stupid
fairy for **Terminator Gladiator**.

Henry piled extra decorations on
to the branches. Soon the Christmas
tree was so covered in baubles and
tinsel there was barely a hint of green.

357

No one would notice the missing
chocolates. Then Henry stood on
a chair, **dumped** the fairy and,
standing on his TIPPY-TIPPY TOES,

hung **Terminator
Gladiator** at
the top
where he
belonged.
Perfect,
thought
Horrid Henry,
jumping off the chair and stepping
back to admire his work. Absolutely

perfect. Thanks to me this is the best tree ever.

There was a **TERRIBLE** creaking sound. Then another. Then **SUDDENLY** . . .

CRASH!

The Christmas tree toppled over.

Horrid Henry's heart stopped.

Upstairs he could hear Mum and Dad stirring.

"Oy! Who's down there?" shouted Dad.

RUN!!! thought Horrid Henry. Run for your life!!

Horrid Henry ran like he had never run before, up the stairs to his room before Mum and Dad could catch him. Oh please let him get there in time. His parents' bedroom door opened just as Henry dashed inside his room. He'd made it.

He was safe.

SPLASH! The bucket of
water spilled all over him.

TRIP! Horrid Henry fell over the
skipping rope.

CRASH! SMASH!

RING! RING! jangled the bells.

PLLLLLLL! belched the **WHOOPEE** cushions.

"WHAT IS GOING ON IN HERE?" shrieked Mum, glaring.

"Nothing," said Horrid Henry, as he lay sprawled on the floor, soaking wet and tangled up in threads and wires and rope. "I heard a noise downstairs so I got up to check," he added innocently.

"Tree's fallen over," called Dad. "Must have been overloaded. Don't worry, I'll sort it."

"Get back to bed, Henry," said
Mum wearily. "And don't touch your
stocking till morning."

Henry *looked*. And **gasped**. His
stocking was stuffed and bulging.
That **MEAN OLD SNEAK**, thought Horrid
Henry indignantly. How did he do it?
How had he escaped the traps?

Watch out, Father
christmas, thought Horrid
Henry. I'll get you next
year.

HORRID HENRY'S

CHRISTMAS LUNCH

25 December
(at last!)

"Oh, handkerchiefs, just what I wanted," said Perfect Peter. "Thank you so much."

"Not handkerchiefs again," moaned **Horrid Henry**, throwing the hankies aside and **RIPPING** the paper off the next present in his pile.

"Don't **TEAR** the wrapping paper!" squeaked Perfect Peter.

Horrid Henry *ripped* open the present and **groaned**.

YUCK (a pen, pencil and ruler). **YUCK** (a dictionary). **YUCK** (gloves). OK (£15 — should have been a lot more). **Eeew** (a pink bow tie from Aunt Ruby). **Eeew** (mints). **YUM** (huge tin of chocolates). **GOOD** (five more knights for his army). **VERY GOOD** (a subscription to *Gross-Out* Fan Club) . . .

And (**VERY VERY GOOD**) a **Terminator Gladiator** trident . . . and . . .

And . . . where was the rest?

"**IS THAT IT?**" shrieked Henry.

"You haven't opened my present, Henry," said Peter. "I hope you like it."

Horrid Henry tore off the wrapping. It was a *Manners With Maggie* calendar.

"**Ugh, gross**," said Henry. "No thank you."

"Henry!" said Mum. "That's no way to receive a present."

"I don't care," moaned Horrid Henry. "Where's my **Zapatron Hip-Hop Dinosaur?** And where's the rest of the **Terminator Gladiator** fighting kit? I wanted everything,

not just the trident."

"Maybe next year," said Mum.

"BUT I WANT IT NOW!"

howled Henry.

"Henry, you know that I want doesn't get," said Peter. "Isn't that right, Mum?"

"It certainly is," said Mum. "And I haven't heard you say THANK YOU, Henry."

Horrid Henry *glared* at Peter and sprang. He was a **HORNET**

stinging a **worm** to death.

"WAAAAAAH!" wailed Peter.

"Henry! Stop it or—"

DING! DONG!

"They're here!" shouted Horrid Henry, leaping up and abandoning his prey. "That means **more presents!**"

"Wait, Henry," said Mum.

But too late. Henry *raced* to the door and flung it open.

There stood Granny and Grandpa, PRISSY POLLY, PIMPLY PAUL and Vomiting Vera.

"GIMME MY PRESENTS!" he shrieked, snatching a bag of brightly wrapped gifts out of Granny's hand and spilling them on the floor. Now, where were the ones with his name on?

"Merry Christmas, everyone," said Mum brightly. "Henry, don't be rude."

"I'm not being **RUDE**," said Henry. "I just want my presents. Great, money!" said Henry, beaming. "Thanks, Granny! But couldn't you add a few pounds and—"

"Henry, don't be **horrid!**" snapped Dad.

"Let the guests take off their coats," said Mum.

"**Blecccch**,"  said Vomiting Vera, throwing up on Paul.

"**EEEEEK**," said Polly.

All the grown-ups gathered in the sitting room to open their gifts.

"Peter, thank you so much for the perfume, it's my favourite," said Granny.

"I know," said Peter.

"And what a lovely comic, Henry," said Granny. "**Mutant Max** is my . . . um . . . favourite."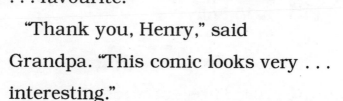

"Thank you, Henry," said Grandpa. "This comic looks very . . . interesting."

"I'll have it back when you've finished with it," said Henry.

"**HENRY!**" said Mum, glaring.

For some reason **POLLY** didn't look

delighted with
her present.

"EEEEK!"
squeaked Polly.
"This soap
has . . . HAIRS in
it." She pulled out
a long black one.

"That came free," said Horrid
Henry.

"We're getting you TOOTHPASTE next
year, you little brat," muttered
PIMPLY PAUL under his breath.

Honestly, there was no pleasing

some people, thought **Horrid Henry** indignantly. He'd given Paul a **GREAT** bar of soap, and he didn't seem thrilled. So much for "it's the thought that counts".

"A poem," said Mum. "Henry, how lovely."

"Read it out loud," said Grandpa.

"Dear old wrinkly Mum
Don't be glum
'Cause you've got a fat tum
And an even bigger . . ."

376

"Maybe later," said Mum.

"Another poem," said Dad. "Great!"

"Let's hear it," said Granny.

"Dear old baldy Dad—

. . . and so forth," said Dad, folding Henry's poem quickly.

"Oh," said Polly, staring at the **crystal frog vase** Mum and Dad had given her. "How funny. This looks just like the vase

I gave Aunt Ruby for Christmas
last year."

"What a coincidence,"
said Mum, blushing
bright red.

"Great minds
think alike," said Dad
quickly.

Dad gave Mum an **IRON**.

"Oh, an **IRON**, just what
I always wanted," said Mum.

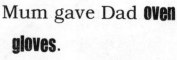

Mum gave Dad **oven
gloves**.

"Oh, **oven gloves**, just

what I always wanted," said Dad.

PIMPLY PAUL gave PRISSY POLLY a **HUGE** *power drill*.

"EEEEK," squealed Polly. "What's this?"

"Oh, that's the *Megawatt Superduper Drill-o-matic 670 XM3*," said Paul, "and just wait till you see the attachments. You're getting those for your birthday."

"Oh," said Polly.

Granny gave Grandpa a lovely mug to put his **false teeth** in.

Grandpa gave Granny a shower cap and a bumper pack of DUSTERS.

"What SUPER presents!" said Mum.

"Yes," said Perfect Peter. "I loved every single one of my presents, especially the satsumas and walnuts in my stocking."

"I didn't," said Horrid Henry.

"Henry, don't be HORRID," said Dad. "Who'd like a mince pie?"

"Are they homemade or from the

380

shop?" asked Henry.

"Homemade, of course," said Dad.

"**GROSS**," said Henry.

"Ooh," said Polly. "No, Vera!" she squealed as Vera **vomited** all over the plate.

"Never mind," said Mum tightly. "There's more in the kitchen."

Horrid Henry was **BORED**. Horrid Henry was **FED UP**. The presents had all been opened. His parents had made him go on a long, boring walk.

Dad had confiscated his **Terminator** trident when he had speared Peter with it.

So, what now?

Grandpa was sitting in the armchair with his pipe, snoring, his *tinsel* crown slipping over his face.

PRISSY POLLY and PIMPLY PAUL were squabbling over whose turn it was to change Vera's *stinky* nappy.

"Eeeek," said Polly. "I did it last."

"I did," said Paul.

"*WAAAAAAAAA!*" wailed Vomiting Vera.

Perfect Peter was watching *Sammy the Snail* slithering about on TV.

Horrid Henry **SNATCHED** the clicker and switched channels.

"Hey, I was watching that!" protested Peter.

"Tough," said Henry.

Let's see, what was on? "*Tra la la la . . .*" Ick! *Daffy and her Dancing Daisies.*

"Wait! I want to watch!" wailed Peter.

CLICK. ". . . and the tension builds as the judges compare tomatoes grown . . ." **CLICK!**

". . . wish you a Merry Christmas, we wish you . . ."
CLICK!

"Chartres Cathedral is one of the wonders of . . ." **CLICK!**

"HA HA HA HA HA HA HA HA." Opera! **CLICK!** Why was there nothing good on TV? Just a baby movie about singing cars he'd seen a million times already.

"**I'm bored**," moaned Henry. "And I"m **STARVING**." He wandered into the kitchen, which looked like a *hurricane* had swept through.

"When's lunch? I thought we were eating at two. I'm **STARVING**."

"Soon," said Mum. She looked a little *frazzled*. "There's been a little problem with the oven."

"**So when's lunch?**" bellowed Horrid Henry.

"When it's ready!" bellowed Dad.

Henry **WAITED**. And **WAITED**. And
WAITED.

"When's lunch?" asked Polly.

"When's lunch?" asked Paul.

"When's lunch?" asked Peter.

"As soon as the turkey is cooked,"
said Dad. He peeked into the oven. He
poked the turkey. Then he went pale.

"It's hardly cooked," he whispered.

"Check the temperature," said
Granny.

Dad checked.

"Oops," said Dad.

"Never mind, we can start with the **sprouts**," said Mum cheerfully.

"That's not the right way to do **sprouts**," said Granny. "You're peeling too many of the leaves off."

"Yes, Mother," said Dad.

"That's not the right way to make bread sauce," said Granny.

"Yes, Mother," said Dad.

"That's not the right way to make **STUFFING**," said Granny.

"Yes, Mother," said Dad.

"That's not the right way to roast potatoes," said Granny.

"**MOTHER!**" yelped Dad. "Leave me alone!"

"Don't be **HORRID**," said Granny.

"I'm not being horrid," said Dad.

"Come along, Granny, let's get you a nice drink and leave the chef on his own," said Mum, steering Granny firmly towards the sitting room. Then she stopped.

"Is something **BURNING**?" asked Mum, sniffing.

Dad checked the oven.

"Not in here."

There was a **SHRIEK** from the sitting room.

"It's Grandpa!" shouted Perfect Peter.

Everyone ran in.

There was Grandpa, asleep in his chair. A thin column of black smoke rose from the arms. His paper crown, drooping over his pipe, was smoking.

"Whh . . . whh?" mumbled Grandpa, as Mum **whacked** him with her broom. "**AAARRGH!**" he gurgled as Dad threw water over him.

"**WHEN'S LUNCH?**" screamed Horrid

Henry.

"**WHEN IT'S READY**," screamed Dad.

It was dark when Henry's family

finally sat down to Christmas lunch.

Henry's tummy was **rumbling** so

loudly with hunger he thought the

walls would cave in. Henry and Peter

made a *dash* to grab the seat against

the wall, furthest from the kitchen.

"**Get off!**" shouted Henry.

"It's my turn to sit here," wailed Peter.

"Mine!"

"Mine!"

Slap!
Slap!

"**WAAAAAAAAAAA!**" screeched Henry.

"WAAAAAAAAAAA!" wailed Peter.

"Quiet!" screamed Dad.

Mum brought in fresh holly and ivy to decorate the table.

"Lovely," said Mum, placing the

boughs all along the centre.

"Very festive," said Granny.

"I'M STARVING!" wailed Horrid Henry. "This isn't Christmas **LUNCH**, it's Christmas **DINNER**."

"Shhh," said Grandpa.

The turkey was finally cooked. There were platefuls of **stuffing**, *sprouts*, cranberries, **BREAD SAUCE** and peas.

"Smells good," said Granny.

"Hmmn, boy," said Grandpa. "What a feast."

Horrid Henry was so hungry he could eat the tablecloth.

"Come on, let's eat!" he said.

"Hold on, I'll just get the roast potatoes," said Dad. Wearing his new oven gloves, he carried in the **steaming hot** potatoes in a glass roasting dish and set it in the middle of the table.

"Voilà!" said Dad.

"Now, who wants dark
meat and who . . ."

"What's that crawling
. . . aaaarrrghh!"
screamed Polly.
"There are **SPIDERS**
everywhere!"
Millions of TINY
SPIDERS were
pouring from the
holly and Crawling
all over the table and the food.

"Don't panic!" shouted Pimply Paul,
leaping from his chair. "I know what

to do, we just—"

But before he could do anything,
the glass dish with the roast
potatoes exploded.

CRASH!

SMASH!

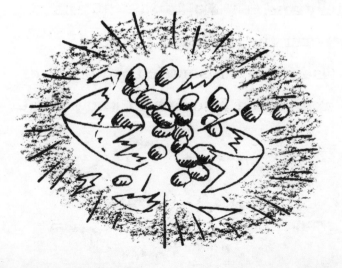

"EEEEEKK!" screamed Polly.

Everyone stared at the slivers of glass glistening all over the table and the food.

Dad sank down in his chair and covered his eyes.

"Where are we going to get more food?" whispered Mum.

"I don't know," muttered Dad.

"I know," said Horrid Henry, "let's start with Christmas pudding and defrost some pizzas."

Dad opened his eyes.

Mum opened her eyes.

"That," said Dad, "is a **BRILLIANT** idea."

"I really fancy some **pizza**," said Grandpa.

"Me too," said Granny.

Henry *beamed*. It wasn't often his ideas were recognised for their brilliance.

"Merry christmas, everyone," said Horrid Henry. "Merry christmas."

COLLECT ALL THE
HORRID HENRY STORYBOOKS!